DON

SEA DEVILS

DOCTOR WHO AND THE SEA-DEVILS

Based on the B.B.C. television serial *The Sea-Devils*
by Malcolm Hulke by arrangement with
the British Broadcasting Corporation

MALCOLM HULKE

Illustrated by
ALAN WILLOW

A TARGET BOOK
published by
the Paperback Division of
W. H. ALLEN & Co. Ltd

A Target Book
Published in 1974
by the Paperback Division of W. H. Allen & Co. Ltd
A Howard & Wyndham Company
44 Hill Street, London W1X 8LB

Second impression 1979
Third impression 1980

Printed in Great Britain by The Anchor Press Ltd
Tiptree, Essex

ISBN 0 426 11308 X

CONTENTS

I

'Abandon Ship!'

'Abandon ship! Abandon ship!'

Second Officer Mason could hear the Captain's voice coming from every loudspeaker on the ship as he worked his way along the upper deck. A huge sea was sending waves and spray over the decks: a Force Nine gale was blowing in from the south west, and now, almost unbelievably, it seemed the bottom had been ripped out of the ship. She was lurching badly to port, poised to vanish any moment beneath the huge waves. Mason pulled his way along a handrail until he came across some of the engine-room crew; they were desperately trying to lower one of the lifeboats.

'Where's Jock?!' he called, yelling above the noise of the crashing waves. 'And where's the Jamaican?'

One of the engine-room men, nicknamed The Scouse, yelled back to Mason: 'They're dead! They're both dead!'

Mason could not believe the men were dead. Only two hours ago, before he turned in for the night, he had been drinking cocoa with the Jamaican. The Jamaican, who really came from Trinidad and had never been to Jamaica in his life, had shown Mason a letter from his mother who lived in a town called St. James. 'It's carnival next month,' said the Jamaican, 'and she wants her best-looking son back home for Carnival—and that's me!' He had saved his air fare, and was booked on a flight from London Airport three days after the s.s. *Pevensey Castle* got into the Port of London, where she was bound. And now the Jamaican, and Jock, and goodness knew how many others, were all dead.

Mason struggled over to help the men from the engine-room lower the lifeboat. He had the greatest respect for engineers when they were in the engine-rooms, but he was not impressed with their upperdeck seamanship.

'Steady there!' he shouted, and took one of the winches himself. There were four men on the winches, and five men huddled in the boat. Under Mason's guidance, the lifeboat was evenly lowered into the boiling sea.

'Abandon ship! Abandon ship!'

The Captain's voice again boomed out over the loud-speakers. Mason wondered whether the Captain intended to stay on his bridge giving out the order to abandon ship until there was no ship left to abandon. Traditionally a ship's captain was supposed to be the last man on board if the ship was sinking, and some captains had been known to stay on the bridge beyond the margin of safety, and to die as a result. Mason hoped his captain would be sensible, and get into one of the lifeboats while there was still a chance.

The Scouse called into Mason's ear: 'She's hit water!'

Mason looked down. The lifeboat was now riding on the sea, and the men down there were letting loose the davit ropes. He cupped his hands to his mouth and called down to them, 'Get rowing—pull away! Pull away!'

But the men in the lifeboat did not need to be told. They all knew that when a big ship finally sinks, she will drag with her any small craft standing close by. They had their oars out, and they were rowing frantically. Then the smoke started to rise from their little boat. Mason stared in horror as thick black smoke burst from the woodwork by the men's feet. Within moments the whole bottom of the inside of the lifeboat started to glow with the redness of fire that was coming up from the sea beneath the little boat!

The Scouse and the other engine-room men looked down at the stricken lifeboat. 'It must have had petrol in its bottom,' said the Scouse, his voice choking and barely audible against the gale, 'and one of them's dropped a lighted cigarette.'

Mason did not believe this, but said nothing. With the spray and the waves it would be impossible for any man to smoke a cigarette, or even for loose petrol to ignite.

8

He sensed that what he was witnessing had no explanation that would ever be known to himself or to the men around him. The whole lifeboat had by now burst into flames, that defied all the seawater, and the five occupants had tumbled overboard.

'Lifebelts!' Mason shouted. 'We can throw them lifebelts!'

Two of the engine-room men struggled along the lurching deck to get lifebelts. But they were not going to save the five men now struggling desperately in the water. As Mason and the Scouse watched, one of the bobbing bodies abruptly disappeared under the water, as though grabbed and pulled down. There was a brief underwater struggle, evidenced by bubbles and foam—then nothing.

'Sharks!' said the Scouse. 'Killer sharks!'

Mason did not bother to argue. Killer sharks do not use underwater blow-lamps, don't set fire to lifeboats. Killer sharks do not lurk in the waters off the coast of southern England. Mason grabbed the handrail and pulled himself up the steeply sloping deck towards the radio-room. As he left the Scouse, who stood staring at the men in the water, another man was savagely pulled under. By now Mason knew that they were all doomed . . . the ship would be gone in another minute, and every man who got into a lifeboat, or into the sea, was going to meet the same fate as the men he'd already seen go down.

The stricken vessel was almost on its side as Mason yanked open the door of the radio-room. Sparks, as they had all called him, was still at his post, calling urgently into a microphone:

'*May Day, May Day! This is s.s. Pevensey Castle. We are abandoning ship!*'

'Give me the microphone,' ordered Mason. He reached out and took the microphone from Sparks.

'*We are being attacked!*' Mason screamed into the microphone. '*The bottom of our ship has been ripped out. Men are being pulled down into the sea—*'

Mason stopped abruptly and stared at the Sea-Devil now standing in the doorway. It had the general shape of

9

a man, yet its body was covered in green scales, and the face was that of a snout-nosed reptile.

'Sea-lizards,' said Sparks, seeking some explanation, however unscientific, for the creature standing before them.

The Sea-Devil turned its head and looked at Sparks, as though it had understood what he said. Then it raised its right paw, and Mason saw that it carried a highly sophisticated weapon—a sort of gun.

'You're intelligent,' said Mason, 'you understand. You're not an animal at all!' For a brief moment Mason had hopes that this thing, whatever it was, might be there to save them. It was, literally, the hope of a drowning man clutching for a straw in the water.

The Sea-Devil killed Sparks first, then Mason. No trace of them, or of the s.s. *Pevensey Castle*, would ever be found – except for one empty lifeboat that the Sea-Devils somehow failed to destroy completely.

2

Visitors for the Master

Jo Grant definitely felt sea-sick. She had travelled through Time and Space with the Doctor in the TARDIS, but that was very much more comfortable than sitting, as she was now, in a small open fishing-boat with a noisy outboard motor. It wasn't only the motion of the boat that made her feel ill : the fast-revving little motor was blowing off petrol fumes that a slight breeze blew straight into her face, and the water they were crossing had on it slicks of oil, occasional dead fish, empty bobbing plastic milk bottles, and some rather unpleasant-looking items that may have come direct from the main sewer.

The Doctor leaned towards Jo, shouting above the noise of the little engine. 'Feeling all right?'

She nodded. 'Fine,' she said, without much enthusiasm. 'When do we get there?'

'As the porcupine said to the turtle,' shouted the Doctor, ' "When we get there" '. It sounded like a quotation from *Alice in Wonderland*, but Jo suspected the Doctor had just made it up. The Doctor turned to the boatman, a Mr. Robbins, and shouted at him : 'Is it in sight, yet?'

The boatman nodded and pointed with a rather dirty finger. Jo looked towards the island to which they were heading, and now, as they rounded a headland, she could see a very large isolated house, something on the lines of a French château. 'That's where they got him,' Robbins shouted. 'It's a disgrace, if you ask me.'

'Not large enough?' said the Doctor, trying to make a joke.

Robbins shook his head, taking the Doctor seriously. 'If you ask me,' he shouted, 'if you really wants my opinion, as an ordinary man in the street, as a taxpayer that's got to pay for all the guards and everything, I'll tell you what they should have done.' He drew a finger swiftly across his throat. '*That's* what he deserved.'

Mr. Robbins, the boatman, was expressing a widely-held view as to what should have happened to the Master. It was not without reason. Through Doctor Who, Jo had known about the Master for some time. She had been with the Doctor, a thousand years into the future and on another planet, when the Master had tried to take control of the Doomsday Weapon in his quest for universal power. More recently the Master had brought himself directly to the attention of the public on Earth by his efforts to conspire with dæmons, using psionic science to release the powers of a monster called Azal.[1] It was this that had brought about his downfall. He had been finally trapped and arrested by Brigadier Lethbridge Stewart of the United Nations Intelligence

[1] See DOCTOR WHO AND THE DÆMONS

Taskforce—UNIT—and put on trial at a special Court of Justice. Although the horror of capital punishment had long been established in Great Britain, many people had wanted to see the Master put to death. To the amazement of the Brigadier, however, the Doctor had made a personal plea to the Court for the Master's life to be spared. Naturally the Doctor could not explain in public that both he and the Master were not really of this planet, and that at one time both had been Time Lords. No Court would have believed him! But in his plea the Doctor talked of the Master's better qualities—his intelligence, and his occasional wit and good humour. Jo well-remembered the Doctor's final words to the Judges: 'My Lords, I beg you to spare the prisoner's life, for by so doing you will acknowledge that there is always the possibility of redemption, and that is an important principle for us all. If we do not believe that anyone, even the worst criminal, can be saved from wickedness, then in what can we ever believe?' After six hours of private discussion the Judges had decided to sentence the Master to life-long imprisonment. They did not realise that, in the case of a Time Lord, 'life-long' might mean a thousand years!

The British authorities had then been faced with a big problem: where was the Master to be imprisoned? Brigadier Lethbridge Stewart had then written a long letter directly to the Prime Minister, trying to explain that the Master was no ordinary prisoner. It was no good putting him in even the most top security prison. For one thing, he had the ability to hypnotise people. Generally, hypnotists can only use their powers over other people who want to be hypnotised; but the Master had only to speak to a potential victim in a certain way, and —unless they were very strong minded—he had them under his spell. The Doctor had also written a long letter to the Prime Minister. He had endorsed the Brigadier's warning, but then added a point of his own. When criminals, even murderers, are sentenced to 'life' imprisonment they usually only serve about ten years; this is because when a judge says 'life' he really means that the length of time in prison can be decided by the Prison Department, depending on a prisoner's good behaviour and chances of leading a good life if he is eventually released. But in the case of the Master, the Judges had specifically said 'life-long', which meant until the Master died of old age. The Doctor, therefore, had asked the Prime Minister to use his compassion and to grant to the Master very considerate treatment. 'The Master's loss of freedom,' the Doctor had written, 'will be punishment enough. I suggest that in your wisdom you create a special prison for him, where he will be able to live in reasonable comfort, and where he will have the opportunity to pursue his intellectual interests.'

The Prime Minister had taken the advice of both the Brigadier and the Doctor. At enormous expense, a huge château on an off-shore island had been bought by the Government and turned into a top security prison—for just one prisoner. What the Prime Minister had done may have been right and proper, but it had cost taxpayers like Mr. Robbins the boatman a great deal of money. So, many people like Mr. Robbins—millions of them—had good reason to feel that the Master should have been put to death, and as quickly as possible.

The little open fishing-boat had now entered a small harbour. The water was calm here, but twice as polluted with muck. Jo kept her eyes on the quayside, to avoid seeing what floated all around her.

'How long are you going to be?' queried Robbins, as he stopped the engine, letting the boat glide towards the quay.

'Maybe an hour,' said the Doctor. 'Can you wait for us?'

Robbins nodded. 'You'll find me round there somewhere,' and he pointed to a café on the quayside. 'Mind, I'll have to charge extra for waiting.' He produced a long pole with a hook on the end, used it to secure a hold on a metal ring set in the cobblestones on the quayside. 'Can you make us up?'

The Doctor jumped on to the quayside, and Robbins threw him a line. The Doctor made fast the rope to the metal ring, then reached out to help Jo from the boat. Glad to be on firm land again, she looked across the murky water of the little harbour towards the open sea. A couple of miles off-shore was a huge metal construction standing out of the water. Pointing it out she said, 'What's that?'

'English Channel oil,' replied Robbins, as he too now came up onto the quayside. 'That's if they ever find it.'

The Doctor asked, 'How long have they been drilling?'

'Last two years,' said Robbins. 'Ever since they really got North Sea oil going, there's been no stopping them.'

Jo had heard a lot about the possibility of English Channel oil. North Sea oil had started gushing in 1977, making Britain the envy of every other European country. Now the geologists promised even greater reserves of crude oil deep beneath the sea-bed of the English Channel, and oil derricks were becoming a familiar sight all along the South Coast.

The Doctor asked, 'How do we get to the château?'

Robbins looked at the Doctor in the way country people do when a stranger asks a silly question. 'You walks,' he said. 'Shanks's pony. You go that way,' and he pointed along a road that kept to the sea for a few hundred yards, then turned inland.

'As you so rightly put it,' said the Doctor, 'we walks. Come along, Jo.'

The Doctor strode off, and Jo hurried to keep up with him. On glancing back, she saw that Robbins had gone into the one and only café.

'You didn't ask how far it is,' she said.

'Not more than a mile,' said the Doctor, striding along on his long legs. 'Well, maybe two . . . Lovely day, don't you think?'

There was a sharp nip in the ozone-laden air blowing in from the sea, and Jo was cold. Not only that, she hadn't put on walking shoes, because she hadn't expected to have to walk two miles to the château and then, presumably, two miles back. 'Marvellous,' she replied, 'as long as I don't get pneumonia.'

'Pneumonia isn't all that serious,' observed the Doctor, taking Jo as seriously as Robbins had taken him about the size of the château. 'There was a time when if you humans developed pneumonia it was often fatal. But nowadays, what with all your new medicines, you'd be over it in no time !'

He strode on, then suddenly stopped. By the side of the road there was an ancient moss-covered stone construction with a single water-tap in the middle. 'That's very interesting,' said the Doctor. 'Most interesting, indeed.'

'You often see them,' said Jo. 'They were built before people had water laid on in their houses.'

'I mean the inscription,' the Doctor said. He reached into the capacious pockets of his long frock coat, and produced a little wire brush. It always astounded Jo how many things he could produce from those enormous pockets. He used the little brush to remove some of the moss, revealing words carefully chipped into the stonework. 'Now,' he said, 'read it.'

Two hundred years of wind had worn away the original surface of the stone, making the inscription very difficult to read. Jo had to run her eyes over it more than once before she could make out all the words :

For you who tread this land
Beware the justice hand
Little boats like men
in days of yore,
They come by stealth at night
They come in broad daylight.
Little boats like men—
Beware the shore.

Jo was not impressed. 'It's a poem,' she said. 'Not a very good one either.'

'What does "justice hand" mean?' said the Doctor, more to himself than to Jo.

'I've no idea,' replied Jo. 'Can we keep walking?'

'What? Oh, yes.' The Doctor strode off again, Jo racing to keep up. 'I've heard of the long arm of justice, but not the hand of justice.'

'It didn't say "the hand of justice",' said Jo, feeling a bit warmer now that they were walking again, 'it said "justice hand". Maybe it's Anglo-Saxon or something.' The wind was blowing up more fiercely now, stinging Jo's cheek with grains of sand whipped up from the nearby shore. She turned up her coat collar.

'Anglo-Saxons,' corrected the Doctor, 'did not build water walls, at least not like that one.' He walked on, head down, obviously thinking hard.

'Does it really matter?' Jo said, spitting grains of sand out of her mouth.

'Of course it matters, my dear,' boomed the Doctor. 'Physical exercise without mental exercise is a bore.' He strode on for a full minute without a word. Then his good-looking face lit up with an idea: 'Is it some ghastly pun on "the scales of justice"?!'

'How do you mean?' said Jo, trying to seem interested.

'It's clearly a warning,' said the Doctor, 'but of what we know not. But a warning means that something bad happens to you if you do the wrong thing. That suggests justice of some sort.'

'Where do scales come into it?' said Jo.

The Doctor laughed. 'Oh, I don't know. Fish have scales. So do reptiles. Just a stupid thought.'

By now they were well away from the quayside with its little café and couple of fishermen's cottages. The château was well in sight, and Jo could see that it was set in its extensive grounds, the road turned a little away from the sea at this point, but the remnants of a track forked off here seeming to run straight to the shore. At the fork there was an old-fashioned milestone sunk deep into the grassy edge. The Doctor stopped and looked at it.

'Fascinating,' he said, staring at the ancient marker.

'What's fascinating,' said Jo, 'about an unused old track that leads straight down to the sea?'

'It means,' said the Doctor patiently, 'that this is a bit of shoreline that is receding before the waves.' He produced his little wire brush again and started to clear moss away from the surface of the milestone. 'Did you know that Henry VIII used to stand on the ramparts of Sandown Castle and, as he wrote, "look out across the fields to the sea beyond"?'

'No,' said Jo apologetically, 'I hadn't heard that. I suppose you knew Henry VIII personally when you travelled back through Time?'

'As a matter of fact,' said the Doctor, 'no. I've never met him. But the significance of all that is that not only have those fields disappeared beneath the sea, but Sandown Castle has as well. There!' He had finished his moss-removing work, and now stood back to regard the result.

Jo could now clearly read a name inscribed in the stone. 'So once upon a time,' she said, 'down that track, before the land sank and let in more of the sea, there was a place called'—she screwed up her eyes to read the name —'Belial Village. So what?'

' "So what?" ' exclaimed the Doctor, pretending to be shocked. 'That's an out-dated Americanism.'

'I picked it up watching old movies on television,' said Jo. 'So what?'

'Well,' said the Doctor, pocketing his little wire brush, 'it just strikes me as interesting.'

'Everything,' said Jo, 'strikes you as interesting—and I am cold, rather hungry, and there are grains of sand in my eyes, nostrils, mouth, and now leaking down my neck. What is interesting about a village which must have been washed away by the sea hundreds of years ago?'

'Belial is a name for the Devil, don't you see?' he said. 'But even more, it was the name used by your poet Milton for one of the fallen angels.'

Jo got the point. The coincidence made her forget all

17

her physical discomforts. 'The Master is a sort of fallen Time Lord!'

'Exactly,' affirmed the Doctor. 'Now, shall we go and pay him a visit?'

After another twenty minutes of hard trudge along the country road, the Doctor and Jo arrived at the gates to the grounds of the château. It was easy to see that big changes had taken place on account of the Master. A wall about four feet tall ran along the entire perimeter of the vast grounds, as far as the eye could see. Little nubs of metal stood up from the wall at regular intervals evidence that in earlier times it had been surmounted by wrought-iron railings. Jo remembered being told that during the Second World War almost all fences and railings in Britain were taken by the Government because of the desperate need for all types of metal to make guns, ships, and bombs. Many old buildings had never had their railings replaced; here, however, a brand new electrified fence had been built on the inside of the old wall. The actual gates, however, were clearly the originals; indeed, some metal gates of supposedly excellent workmanship were spared during the war. They stood about twelve feet high, set between huge stone uprights. But now one of the gates had had a big notice screwed to it, the warning you see outside any of Her Majesty's prisons: in rather stilted English it solemnly warned the visitor of the punishments they might receive if they helped, assisted, or encouraged any prisoner in an attempt to escape. Almost hidden among the nightmare of Victorian iron-work was a small push-button for a bell.

The Doctor put his finger to it, and pushed.

A gatekeeper's cottage stood just to one side of the drive on the other side of the gates. Jo saw a uniformed prison officer come from the cottage towards them.

'What is it?' The prison officer stood a few feet from the gates and made no attempt to open them.

'We've called to visit the prisoner,' the Doctor shouted back.

The prison officer remained where he was. 'Got your VO's?'

'Got our what?' said the Doctor.

Jo quickly fished in a pocket and produced their two special visitor's papers issued to the Doctor by the Ministry of the Interior. She held them through the gates. 'We haven't got Visitors' Orders,' Jo explained, 'but these were issued by the Minister himself.'

Now the prison officer came forward and carefully examined the two passes. 'Got anything to identify yourselves?'

Jo handed in their two UNIT passes. 'The Doctor actually helped to catch the prisoner,' she said, pointedly.

'Really?' said the prison officer and continued mildly, 'and I'm the Lord Mayor of London.' He produced a key from his extraordinarily long key chain and unlocked the gates. The moment Jo and the Doctor had stepped inside, the prison officer locked the gates behind them. 'Keep within two paces of me,' he ordered, and started walking towards the gatekeeper's cottage. Just outside it, on the driveway itself, was a wooden sentry-box. Within was a telephone which the prison officer now lifted. He dialled two digits and waited for an answer. 'Gatehouse here, sir,' he said. 'Two visitors for the prisoner, sir. They have identified themselves as UNIT personnel, and they have authority to make the visit from the Minister.' He listened for a moment. 'Yes, sir. Right away, sir.' He put down the 'phone, put two fingers into his mouth and whistled. Like a jack-in-the-box another prison officer came hurrying out of the cottage.

'These two for the château,' said the first prison officer. 'Jump to it.'

The other officer wheeled about, and disappeared round the side of the cottage. A moment later he came back, driving a Minimoke.

'Show him your passes,' said the first prison officer, 'and he'll drive you up there.'

'But we've already shown *you* our passes,' the Doctor protested.

'How is he to know,' said the first prison officer, 'that you and I aren't in a conspiracy to free the prisoner?'

For a second Jo thought the man must be joking, then realised he was deadly serious. She saw that the Doctor was about to explode in wrath against bureaucracy, so to save that she quickly showed their passes to the Minimoke driver.

'Two being passed over to you, Mr. Snellgrove,' announced the first prison officer.

'Am receiving two from you, Mr. Crawley,' said the second prison officer seated at the driving wheel of the Minimoke.

'All right,' said the prison officer called Crawley, 'hop in quick, you two.'

'Well, jump to it,' barked the Doctor, and climbed on board the Minimoke. He talked in the same sergeant-majorish way as the prison officers. 'Am now sitting in Minimoke.'

Prison Officer Crawley crossed over to the Doctor and looked at him with the disdain he normally reserved for criminals in his care. 'All right, sonny. You may think we're a big laugh here. But let me tell you this: the way I look at it, the world's divided into three groups of people—those who have been in prison, those who *are* in prison, and those who will be going to prison. Got it?'

Jo quickly got into the back of the Minimoke next to the Doctor. 'I'm sure we understand perfectly,' she said, 'and thank you for being so kind. Can we go now?'

Prison Officer Crawley turned and went back into the gatekeeeper's cottage without a word. Prison Officer Snellgrove put the Minimoke into gear and drove it, at not more than ten miles per hour, all the way up the drive to the vast Victorian front door of the château.

The door was not opened until Prison Officer Snellgrove had given the right number of knocks. It was then opened by two more prison officers, who immediately wished to see Jo's and the Doctor's passes and UNIT identity cards. The prison officer who had brought them said, 'Two being passed over to you, Mr. Sharp,' and

Prison Officer Sharp, who guarded the front door, replied, 'Am receiving two from you, Mr. Snellgrove.'

As soon as the Doctor and Jo were inside the vast hallway, the front door was closed and locked. Prison Officer Sharp barked at the visitors, 'Keep two paces behind me,' and promptly marched off down a stone corridor, followed by the Doctor and Jo. Sharp eventually stopped at a small door of ornately carved wood with huge wrought-iron hinges. He knocked, entered, and held open the door, and stood to attention.

'Visitors—two,' announced Sharp, staring straight ahead of himself, as though on a parade ground, 'being handed over to you, Mr. Trenchard—sir!'

The Doctor and Jo followed Sharp into the governor's office. It was a big gloomy room with cathedral-like windows, all with bars, and a lot of heavy, brown wood-panelling. The furniture was old-fashioned—a couple of enormous leather armchairs, and a huge old desk. George Trenchard, a retired army officer, was seated at the desk, writing a memorandum. He was a big-built man with a bull neck, middle-aged, dressed in conventional country-gentleman tweed suit and an Old School tie. He remained where he was, writing away, without looking up. Jo and the Doctor waited patiently. Jo was reminded of a rather stupid headmistress she had once known who had always used this technique when girls went in to see her; it was a trick to make visitors feel unsure of themselves. After a while the Doctor cleared his throat, very noisily.

Trenchard spoke, but still without looking up. 'All right, Sharp,' he murmured, 'carry on.'

'Sir!' shrieked Sharp, saluting with force enough to knock his own brains out. He turned on his heel, and left the office. Trenchard continued to write.

'We could always come back later,' said the Doctor helpfully.

Trenchard signed his name to the memorandum and looked up, delivering a perfectly charming Old School smile. 'Ah, yes, you'll be the people from UNIT.' He rose and extended his hand. 'Terribly, terribly glad to see you both.'

Jo shook hands with him. 'I'm Josephine Grant, and this is the Doctor.'

'A Doctor, eh?' said Trenchard. 'I'm getting a few twinges these days. Must be old-age creeping on. Still, don't want to bother you while you're out for a day. You're late, you know.'

'We had difficulty getting a boat to bring us across,' explained Jo.

'Ah, that old problem,' said Trenchard. 'But I thought you might have sunk without trace.'

'During a two-mile crossing from the mainland?' said the Doctor, scathingly.

'Two miles or two hundred miles,' said Trenchard, 'it has happened a lot recently.'

'What has?' The tone in the Doctor's voice clearly hinted to Jo his distaste for Trenchard.

'Ships vanishing,' said Trenchard. 'Still, that's the modern world for you.' Before the Doctor could ask him what on Earth he was talking about, Trenchard continued: 'Got your passes?'

'We've been through all that,' said the Doctor. 'That's how we're in this room.'

Trenchard grinned. 'Don't take any chances here, old man. Let's see them.'

Jo produced the passes and Trenchard checked them carefully. He handed them back to her. 'Seem to be in order. You'll be wanting to see the prisoner, I shouldn't wonder.'

'That,' said the Doctor, with forced patience, 'is the general idea.'

'Jolly interesting fellow,' remarked Trenchard. 'His intelligence is a bit above the ordinary criminal type, you know. Pity, really, that a man of his ability should have got himself into this fix.'

'What I'd like to know,' said the Doctor, 'is whether he's tried to get himself *out* of this fix? Has he tried to hypnotise any of your guards?'

'He couldn't.' Trenchard beamed at them both. 'Every man here is completely immune to hypnotism. They've all been checked out by these trick-cyclist people.'

'Trick-cyclists?' said the Doctor, taking Trenchard quite literally.

'Psycho-analysts,' whispered Jo.

'Like to see a demonstration?' said Trenchard. 'Just watch this.' He turned to two huge oak cupboard doors and opened them. Inside was a panel that included a television monitor screen, loudspeaker and a flush microphone with controls. He pressed one of the controls and shouted at the top of his voice into the microphone, as though he did not really believe that electronics could carry sound. '*Trenchard here. Send that new man, Wilson, in to see the prisoner.*' Then he pressed another button, and instantly there was a picture on the monitor screen. It showed the Master seated reading in a very pleasant room.

'He's putting on weight,' commented the Doctor.

'I know,' said Trenchard. 'Poor chap. Can't get the exercise, you see. Now watch this.'

On the screen they saw a prison officer enter the Master's room. The Master looked up. 'Yes?'

'Mr. Trenchard sent me, sir, to know if you wanted your book changed,' said the prison officer.

'That's very kind of him,' said the Master. 'But I haven't quite finished this one. You're new here, aren't you?'

'Yes, sir,' said the prison officer. 'The name's Wilson.'

'Well, Mr. Wilson,' said the Master cordially, 'I hope we shall be friends.' Suddenly, the Master's friendly expression changed, and his dark brown eyes stared straight into Wilson's eyes. 'I am the Master and you will obey me.'

'I knew it,' said Jo. 'I knew he'd be up to his old tricks.'

'Please, Miss Grant,' said Trenchard, 'just watch what happens.'

The Master and Prison Officer Wilson were now look-

ing into each other's eyes. 'You will obey me,' command-
ed the Master. 'Do you understand?'

Wilson smiled. 'You just let me know when you've
finished your book, sir,' he said, 'and I'll get you another.'
With that Wilson turned and left the room. For a few
seconds the Master stared at the now closed door, then
sunk back in despair to where he had been sitting, and
soon started to read his book again.

'Most impressive,' agreed the Doctor. 'May we now
see him in person?'

'Certainly,' said Trenchard. 'I'll lead the way.' He
picked up a rather old-fashioned pork-pie hat, popped
it on to his greying head, and led the Doctor and Jo out
of the office. They went down a brightly-lit stone staircase to the vast basement of the château, and then along
a corridor. Finally, they came to a steel door set in the
stone wall, where a prison officer—this one possessed of
a gun—stood to attention as Trenchard arrived.

'At ease,' said Trenchard, 'and open up, there's
a good fellow.'

The Master was not reading when Jo and the Doctor
entered; instead he had turned to getting some much
needed exercise on a shiny new rowing machine. The
room was quite large, fitted out with modern furniture,
wall-to-wall carpeting, and a colour television set. There
was no bed, but let into the opposite wall there was a
door, so Jo concluded the Master had another room beyond which was his sleeping-quarters. A slight humming
sound indicated the presence of air-conditioning.

The Master glanced up from this rowing machine.
'Why, Doctor—and Miss Grant. What a pleasant surprise!' He seemed quite genuinely pleased to see them,
and scrambled up from the rowing machine to shake
hands.

'Bit of a surprise for you, eh?' said Trenchard, very
full of himself. 'Naturally I knew they were coming, but
didn't tell you in case they didn't make it. Didn't want
you to suffer a disappointment.'

'That was very thoughtful of you,' said the Master

appreciatively. He turned back to regard the Doctor again. 'It really *is* good to see you, Doctor.'

'Well,' said the Doctor, not a little touched by the Master's obvious joy at the visit, 'how are you?'

The Master pointed to the rowing machine. 'Trying to keep fit, you know.'

Compared with the Doctor, the Master seemed completely at his ease.

Trenchard realised he was not really welcome during this reunion of old enemies. 'I'll leave you all together,' he said, putting on a smile. 'Give a shout to the guard when you want to leave.' And with that he hurried out, and the door was closed and locked behind him.

'I'm afraid I can't offer you any refreshments,' apologised the Master, 'but do sit down.'

They did as he asked. Jo thought it was rather like people saying goodbye at a railway station, when no one knows what to say. The Master broke the silence.

'He's not a bad sort, really,' he said, indicating the door through which Trenchard had just retreated. 'He was the governor of some British colony before this, so he tells me.'

'Yes, so I heard,' said the Doctor, glad to have something to talk about. 'The colony claimed its independence soon after he arrived.'

Jo said, 'He seems to be looking after you all right.'

The Master turned to her. 'I have everything I want, Miss Grant. Except, of course, my freedom.'

'You were lucky to get away with your life,' said the Doctor. 'A lot of people wanted you to be executed.'

The Master smiled. 'My dear Doctor, don't think I'm ungrateful.' He paused for a moment. 'As a matter of fact, I've had time to think in here.'

Jo noticed the Doctor's immediate warm reaction to the Master's remark. 'Have you really? I rather hoped that you would.'

'To be honest,' said the Master, 'and I'd only admit this to old friends, I wish something like this had happened to me a long time ago.'

'You're glad to be locked up?' Jo could hardly believe her ears.

'Miss Grant, no one in their right mind is glad to be locked up,' said the Master. 'But a little enforced isolation gives one an opportunity to reconsider what life is all about.' He looked down at his carpeted floor. 'I suppose there's no chance of the British Government ever granting me *parole* from here?'

'The judge ordered life-long imprisonment,' said the Doctor, more forlornly than with any pleasure at the Master's situation.

'He was right, of course,' said the Master. 'I have been thoroughly evil. But we must remember that when I was tried, my wrongdoings were still fresh in people's minds. They felt affronted by what I had done. All I am hoping is that when the dust has, as it were, settled and people are able to think of me with a little less hate, they might be willing to show some humane mercy.'

The Master spoke with such feeling and sincerity that Jo felt very sorry for him. Although this room was comfortable, and was unlike any other cell in a British prison, it seemed to her terrible that anyone should be locked in for the rest of his life. The Doctor also seeemed to be affected by the Master's plea for mercy.

'Don't imagine that I enjoy seeing you detained in this place,' said the Doctor. 'To be honest, it distresses me very much. If the authorities were willing to give you, say, limited freedom, would you be willing to tell me the location of your TARDIS?'

Jo studied the Master's face intently to see his reaction to this vital question. When the Master last came to this planet he had concealed his TARDIS, and at his trial refused to say where it was hidden. The Master smiled.

'So that you, Doctor, could use my TARDIS to leave the planet Earth?' he asked.

Jo had not thought of this. She knew that the Doctor's TARDIS only seemed to work when it wanted to, and that the Doctor had little or no control over it. She looked now to see how the Doctor would react.

'No,' he said firmly, 'we want to know where your TARDIS is so that *you* can't leave the planet Earth.'

'But to be logical,' said the Master, 'would it not please the authorities on Earth for me to take off and fly far, far away, where I could not possibly do them any harm?'

Jo cut in: 'I thought you said you had changed your mind about doing bad things any more?'

'Indeed I have, Miss Grant,' said the Master, flashing his most charming and sincere smile. 'But it seems that the authorities will never be convinced of that. All I am hinting at therefore, is that if I were far from this planet, everyone on Earth would be able to sleep in their beds more soundly!'

'My dear old friend,' said the Doctor, 'you know as well as I do that if you were released from here, *and* had access to your TARDIS, Earth would never be safe from the possibility of your returning to it, maybe bringing with you all sorts of unpleasant allies—Ogrons, Daleks, Cybermen, or even more dreadful entities.' He leaned forward to the Master with an earnest expression. 'Believe me, I hate to think of you cooped up in here. It is faintly possible that I could persuade the Government to give you limited freedom, but only if you reveal the whereabouts of your TARDIS—because only then could we really keep an eye on you. Now then, what do you say?'

The Master stroked his beard thoughtfully. Then, slowly, he shook his head. 'I'm sorry, Doctor, it's too much to ask.'

'But what use is your TARDIS to you while you're in here?' Jo asked.

'It would be difficult for you to understand,' said the Master, 'but my TARDIS is my proudest possession.'

The Doctor laughed. 'You don't even own it! You stole it from the Time Lords!'

'As you stole yours!' retorted the Master. 'Now please, let's not start to get all moral. I'm not going to render up my TARDIS to anyone.'

'I see.' The Doctor rose to his feet. 'Jo, can you tell the guard we're ready to go, please?'

Jo went to the door and rapped on it.

'Is there anything you need?' asked the Doctor.

'I have most of the necessary comforts,' replied the Master, also rising to bid them farewell. 'But I'd appreciate an occasional chat, if you ever have the time. Trenchard is a decent fellow but his conversation is somewhat limited.'

The prison officer opened the door.

'I shall try to visit you again soon,' said the Doctor. 'In the meantime, if there is anything you want, you know where you can drop a note to me—at UNIT Headquarters.'

'That's most civilised of you,' said the Master. He shook hands with the Doctor, then extended his hand to Jo. 'I appreciate your visit immensely, Miss Grant. You have shown great mercy and compassion towards a defeated enemy.'

There was such sincerity in the Master's voice that Jo felt quite overcome with emotion. 'At least we're not enemies now,' she said a little huskily.

'We are victor and vanquished,' said the Master, 'and I stand humbled before you. Perhaps, in time, the others will come to realise that all I seek now is forgiveness for my sins. Goodbye, Miss Grant, and may God be with you.'

As they left the room, Jo noticed the Master wipe a single tear from his eye.

Back in Trenchard's office, the Doctor stood at the window gazing silently out at the rolling green lawns of the château's estate. He seemed lost in thought.

Jo said, 'Did you really think the Master would tell you where his TARDIS is?'

'Not really,' said the Doctor without turning. 'He's defeated, and knowledge of its location is the only thing he's got to cling on to.'

'Then why,' she asked, 'did we come all the way down here?'

'Goodbye, Miss Grant,' said the Master, 'and may God be with you.'

The Doctor was evasive. 'I thought a trip to the seaside might do us both good.'

'You're really sorry for him, aren't you?' she said. 'You wanted to be sure he was being treated properly.'

'We used to be great friends,' said the Doctor. 'Hundreds of years ago, when we were both young Time Lords, we were inseparable. After all, we had a lot in common.'

'What, for instance?'

He turned to her. 'You know the Golden Rule of the Time Lords—just to sit and watch, but never actually do anything? He and I are different. We wanted to get out into the Universe, to meet other species, to explore.'

'One for good and the other for evil?' said Jo.

'Yes, you could say that.'

The door opened and Trenchard marched in, all smiles, removing his little pork-pie hat. 'Ready for off then? I'd better stamp the passes.'

Jo produced their passes and Trenchard read them all again as though he had never seen them before, then produced a rubber stamp and an ink pad and stamped them. 'Satisfied with how we look after him?'

The Doctor was buried in thought again, but even so turned. 'What? Oh, yes. Just one thing, though, that made me curious . . .'

Trenchard was handing the stamped passes back to Jo, and avoided the Doctor's eyes as he spoke. 'Oh? What's that?'

'The prison officer whom we saw on the monitor screen,' said the Doctor, 'he asked if the Master was ready to change his book yet.'

For the first time Trenchard did not seem completely at ease. 'Well, a prisoner has a right to have something to read, you know.' He seemed to have a sudden idea, one that might take them off the subject of the Master. 'They deprived Sir Thomas More of his books when he was a prisoner of King Henry in the Tower, you know. That was jolly cruel of them. They were a lot of savages in those days.'

But the Doctor was not to be deflected on to a general

conversation about the treatment of prisoners. 'Since he has wall-to-wall carpeting and coloured television, why doesn't he have a library of books down there in his room?'

Trenchard was momentarily thrown by this question. Then he rallied. 'Prison regulations, old chap! Got to keep to the rules, you know.'

'I agree,' said the Doctor. 'It's just that the two things don't seem to fit.'

'If you really want to know,' said Trenchard, as though taking both the Doctor and Jo into a great confidence, 'when they gave me this job I read the rule book from cover to cover. You see, there's nothing to say that a prisoner *mustn't* have the little comforts that we've provided. Therefore I used my own discretion. But there is a rule laid down by the Prison Department about the issue of books to prisoners, so I had to keep to it.'

'Very crafty of you,' said the Doctor with a smile. 'Well, we shall be on our way. It's been most pleasant to meet you, Mr. Trenchard.'

Trenchard summoned the Minimoke to the front door of the château, and within a few minutes the Doctor and Jo were being slowly driven back to the main gates by Prison Officer Snellgrove.

Jo asked, 'What was all that about books?'

Out of Snellgrove's vision, the Doctor put his fingers to his lips to keep Jo quiet. He said, loud enough for Snellgrove to hear: 'I was just glad that they gave him plenty to read, to keep his mind occupied.'

Once outside the big gates, and back on the road leading to the quayside, Jo tried again. 'I still didn't understand your interest in the Master getting books to read.'

'I think Mr. Trenchard may have misread the prison rules,' explained the Doctor. 'A prisoner is allowed three books per fortnight, not one at a time.'

'Does it matter?' asked Jo, hurrying to keep up with the Doctor's long strides.

'I've no idea,' said the Doctor. 'It just struck me as being strange.'

Meanwhile Trenchard was talking to the Master about the incident of Prison Officer Wilson and the book.

'I think we fooled them nicely,' said Trenchard. 'Wouldn't you agree?'

'I hope so,' said the Master, pouring himself a small whisky from the concealed drinks cabinet in his room, and not offering any to Trenchard.

'That hypnotism wheeze really took them in,' Trenchard went on. 'Remember, I was watching them while they were watching you.'

'Let's hope you're right.' The Master raised his glass to Trenchard. 'Cheers. Now, do you *really* think he came here to see me?'

Trenchard was puzzled. 'Why else would he come?'

The Master tried to restrain his impatience with Trenchard. He regarded the prison governor as a fool, but had to be careful not to show it. 'The sinking ships, of course.'

'Oh, *that*,' said Trenchard, as though the recent deaths of a great many mariners was of no importance. 'He didn't seem particularly interested.'

The Master studied Trenchard, forcing himself to hide his low regard for the man's intelligence. 'What do you mean, "he didn't seem particularly interested"? Did he talk about it?'

'He didn't,' said Trenchard. 'But I did just mention it.'

'You did *what*?'

Trenchard laughed foolishly. 'Just to make conversation. No harm done.'

If any harm had been done, there was nothing the Master could do to stop it now. So curbing his anger, he tried to put a good face on it. 'I suppose not,' he said, finishing his whisky. 'When am I going to get these Admiralty charts?'

Trenchard felt on safe ground again, and looked relieved. 'They will be here this afternoon—absolutely for certain.'

'Splendid,' said the Master. 'Time may not be on our side.'

'I fully recognise the urgency of the situation,' said Trenchard. 'You've convinced me of that. Now if you'll excuse me, I really must hurry along.'

'I quite understand,' said the Master. He put down his glass and returned to his rowing machine. As Trenchard was leaving, he looked up and said, 'By the way, Trenchard, do congratulate Prison officer Wilson on his excellent performance during our little charade.'

'I already have done,' said Trenchard. 'As a matter of fact, he confesses that you did in fact nearly hypnotise him. That would have been a laugh, what?!'

'A big laugh,' agreed the Master.

Trenchard hurried out and the door was closed. The Master thought for a moment and then smiled . . . Then he applied himself with vigour to his rowing exercise. For what he planned to do, he had to keep in first-rate physical condition.

3

The Vanished Ships

'All three ships,' said Mr. Robbins, the boatman, 'they just vanished, like they never was there in the first place.'

The Doctor and Robbins were seated in the quayside café having a cup of tea while Jo was away looking for picture postcards.

'I'm afraid that a lot of ships "just vanish",' said the Doctor. 'On average seven ships vanish without trace somewhere in the world every year—they leave a port, and are never seen again.'

'I don't know about any of them,' said Robbins, totally unimpressed by the statistic of marine losses. 'But I do know about these three.'

'Then why didn't I?' said the Doctor thoughtfully.

Robbins was confused. 'Eh?'

'Why didn't I, and millions of other newspaper readers, know about them,' said the Doctor.

Robbins at last got the point. 'It's all been hushed up, see?'

'Why did they go down?'

'That's the mystery, isn't it?' said Robbins. 'It was only the most recent that even sent a radio-message asking for help.'

'Did they say why they were sinking?'

Robbins scratched his head. 'It's all garbled gossip what exactly they said, only I did hear they were screaming out "Bottom of ship ripped out—men pulled into the sea". It sounded a lot of nonsense to me and the rest of the lifeboat men.'

The Doctor looked across the teacups at Robbins with renewed interest. 'You are a lifeboat man?'

'That's right,' said Robbins. 'Almost every able-bodied man on this little island is in the lifeboat.' He continued, 'We went out, of course, but that ship had gone down so fast there wasn't nothing of it left. Except for the lifeboat.'

Now the Doctor was confused. '*Your* lifeboat?'

'No,' said Robbins, 'one of this ship's lifeboats. It was upside down in the water. And I'll tell you a funny thing about it: the underside was all charred, sort of burnt like, in a pattern.'

By now the Doctor was keenly interested in what had been going on just off the shore here over the last couple of months. 'Had the ship been on fire?'

'Don't think so,' said Robbins. 'We'd have seen the flames. That's what made me think it odd, this little lifeboat being charred.'

Robbins went on to say that the Navy had impounded the lifeboat, and now had it at what Robbins called 'the

34

Base'—a top security Naval Base a couple of miles along the coastline of the island.

The Doctor asked, 'How can I get to this Naval Base?'

'On the coast road,' replied Robbins, 'Strike out in the opposite direction to where you went before. Of course, it would be quicker by boat.'

The Doctor took the hint and stood up. 'Then you'd better take me there straight away.'

'Not to the Naval Base!' Robbins protested. 'If I sailed in there, they'd have me in irons.'

The Doctor thought for a moment. Then he looked at his watch. 'All right. But I wonder if you could go and see what's happened to my young friend? She said she was only going away for five minutes to buy some picture postcards.'

Robbins looked at the Doctor in disbelief. 'I don't know where to look for her.' By his voice he suggested that if the Doctor wanted to find her, the Doctor could go and look.

'There must be a picture postcard shop somewhere here,' said the Doctor. 'You live here—you must know where she could have gone. I'd go if it weren't for my leg hurting again. I got wounded in the Crimea.'

'The Crimean War?' said Robbins, astounded because that war took place over a hundred and twenty years ago.

The Doctor shrugged. 'Perhaps it was Gallipoli. Anyway, be a good fellow and go and find her. I'll pay for our cups of tea.'

Without a word Robbins got to his feet and shuffled out. The Doctor went to the counter and settled the bill, and then looked out of the café. Robbins was already out of sight. The Doctor quickly hurried to the quayside, unloosed Robbins' boat, jumped into it, started the noisy little outboard motor, and headed out to sea. An old man on the quayside mending fishing nets looked up but did nothing to stop the Doctor.

Five minutes later Robbins returned to the spot with Jo. He had grumbled all the way. 'All you and that fellow asked me to do was to take you from the mainland and bring you here, and then take you back again, not to go searching in postcard shops—' He stopped dead as he saw that his boat was missing. He called to the man mending nets, 'Where's my boat?'

The net mender looked up : 'A fellow went off with it,' he called, then pointed off to a headland jutting out into the sea. 'He's making for over there.'

'The Naval Base !' Robbins exploded.

'The what?' said Jo.

Robbins dug into the pockets of his overcoat to find something. 'He wanted me to take him to the Naval Base, and I wouldn't. I'm going to get the police.' At last he found what his hands were looking for—a key to a bicycle padlock. He went over to a bicycle chained to a quayside railing, and unlocked the padlock. 'You wait here, Miss,' he told Jo. 'When I come back here with the policeman, he's likely to ask you a few questions about that friend of yours.'

Robbins was about to mount the machine. Jo thought quickly. 'Look!' she called, 'isn't that your boat coming back now? Maybe he only wanted a little joy-ride.' She pointed out to sea.

Robbins propped his bicycle against the railing, and crossed to where Jo was standing. 'Where is it?'

'Over there,' Jo said, pointing. 'If you screw your eyes up you can just see your boat heading back here.'

Robbins screwed up his eyes to look. Jo ran silently towards the railing, jumped on to Robbins's bicycle and started to pedal away furiously.

'Hey !' Robbins shouted. 'Stop thief !'

'I'll bring it back,' Jo cried over her shoulder. Already she was well away from the quayside, and heading for the Naval Base by the coastal road.

.   .   .   .   .

Captain Hart, RN, commanding officer of the Naval Shore Establishment called HMS *Foxglove*, was a worried man. With an excellent service record behind him, and, he hoped, an equally excellent career ahead of him, he did not like having to report that he had failed to find out why three merchant ships had mysteriously sunk within five miles of his headquarters in the past two months. When Doctor Who first came to his notice, he was painfully dictating a letter to a W.R.N. Writer, Jane Blythe. The letter was addressed to their Lordships at the Admiralty, London.

' "*I regret to inform you,*" ' he started, then paused. 'No, change that to *"I very much regret to inform you that as yet our investigations have revealed no clue as to the cause of these sinkings. The charred ship's lifeboat will be sent to our laboratories at Portsmouth for investigation and analysis, and we can only hope that this may answer some of our questions. Meanwhile, we are keeping careful watch . . ."* '

It was at this point that he noticed the Doctor. While dictating the letter he had been standing at the window of his first-floor office, overlooking the concrete roadways, outbuildings and quayside of this most top security Naval base. No one could possibly enter the base without a special pass, unless they came in from the sea. And that's just what had happened. At the captain watched, a fishing-boat with a small outboard motor had zoomed in from the sea, driven by a tall man with a lot of fair hair and a long black frock coat. The man made up the boat, jumped ashore, and within no time was busily inspecting the upturned charred lifeboat which had been left on the quayside.

Jane looked up from her notebook. 'Is something the matter, sir?'

Captain Hart didn't answer. He scooped up a telephone and bellowed into it : '*Master-at-Arms, we have an intruder! Kindly arrest him and bring him to my office immediately!*'

Hart went back to the window to watch, and Jane joined him there. 'Perhaps he's lost,' said Jane.

'Then why,' said Hart, 'did he go straight for the lifeboat? !'

Within seconds of the captain's call to the Master-at-Arms, they saw a petty officer and six ratings bearing down on the stranger. The petty officer yanked the Doctor to his feet. There was a brief exchange of words, and then the Doctor was marched off, hemmed in by the six Naval ratings.

Three minutes later there was a knock on Captain Hart's door, and the Doctor was brought in under escort. Captain Hart was already seated behind his desk to 'receive' the unwanted visitor.

'Intruder found and detained, sir,' said the petty-officer.

'Look, I'm terribly sorry about all this,' the Doctor began, but was allowed to go on no further.

'Are you aware,' said Captain Hart severely, 'that you have trespassed on Government property, and that that is a very serious offence?'

'Actually,' said the Doctor, 'no, because I had not the means to become aware.'

Captain Hart tried to contain his patience. 'There are signs, in very large letters, warning the public to keep out, and you ignored these!'

'I didn't see any signs,' pleaded the Doctor.

Again Hart cut in. 'Because you entered by way of the sea! Obviously, we can't have signs bobbing up and down on the waves.'

'There you are, then,' said the Doctor. 'So the way I arrived, there were no signs to be seen.'

'But you had no right to enter by way of the sea!' thundered Captain Hart.

'Ah,' said the Doctor soothingly, 'but I was not to know that I had no right unless I saw some sign to tell me.'

It was clear that this conversation was going round in circles. The captain noticed the petty-officer trying to suppress a smile.

'All right, petty officer,' said Hart, 'you can carry on.' It was the Naval way of saying that the petty officer was no longer needed.

'Sir!' said the petty officer, as he about-turned and left the office.

'Perhaps,' said the captain, 'you'd be good enough to tell me why you've dropped in on us in this unconventional way?'

'I'd be delighted,' said the Doctor, helping himself to a chair and sitting down. He explained what he had heard about ships sinking, and about the peculiarity of the lifeboat that was charred when no flames had been seen. 'Before I was arrested,' the Doctor explained, 'I had a brief opportunity to look at those burn marks. I was particularly interested in the linear nature of the burns. Let me show you what I mean.' With a winning smile he reached over and helped himself to Jane's notebook and pencil and drew the pattern of the scorch marks that he had just seen on the bottom of the upturned lifeboat. 'You will notice they have a definite shape, like this,' and he drew a number of overlapping circles. 'Those marks could only have been caused by a concentrated beam of heat applied from underneath when the boat was in the water. It was a clear attempt to make sure that there were no survivors.'

The captain glanced at the Doctor's drawing, then turned back to the Doctor. 'May I ask who you are?'

'I'm the Scientific Adviser to UNIT,' said the Doctor.

'And I,' said Captain Hart, 'am Horatio Nelson.'

'Good grief,' said the Doctor, 'I thought you were shot at Trafalgar. Well, my dear fellow, you've lasted pretty well!'

The captain again held down his temper. 'What I mean, sir, is that you are either an impostor, or mad, or both! If you were in any way connected with UNIT you would have arrived here in a proper manner and started by presenting your credentials!'

'My dear fellow,' said the Doctor, 'how thoughtless of me. But if you had wanted to see my credentials, you should have asked for them.'

'All right then,' said Captain Hart. 'Let me see them.'

The Doctor hesitated. 'I never carry them.'

'Then that,' said Captain Hart emphatically, 'is the end of that!' He picked up the telephone again. '*Master-at-Arms kindly come and take away the man in my office. Put him under guard—and then call for the police . . .*' But it seemed that the Master-at-Arms was now telling the captain something, and the captain listened attentively. '*I see*,' he said at last. '*You'd better bring her to my office.*' He cradled the 'phone.

'Something gone wrong?' asked the Doctor. 'Has a mutiny broken out?'

'There's a young lady,' said Captain Hart, 'at the main gate, on a bicycle, with two UNIT passes. So possibly I shall be able to let you go.'

'But I don't want to be let go!' the Doctor protested. A big chart on the wall caught his eye. It showed the island, part of the mainland, the contours of the sea-bed along this stretch of the coast. Oil-rigs, lightships, and danger points were also marked. In addition there were three black stars stuck to the chart, all clustered around one particular oil-rig. The Doctor pointed to the black stars. 'Do those signify where the ships sank?'

'I can't discuss anything with you,' said Captain Hart, 'until I see your pass. Kindly be quiet.'

The Doctor nodded in agreement, and sat absolutely still. The captain went and stood at his window, hands behind his back, like a man on the bridge of a ship. There was a heavy silence until a petty officer knocked on the door and entered with Jo.

'Doctor,' she cried, happy to see him again. 'That Mr. Robbins is very angry with you!'

The Doctor signalled her to keep quiet about Mr. Robbins and the boat. 'This is Captain Hart, my dear. He'd like to see our passes.'

Jo produced them, and Captain Hart inspected them carefully. 'Thank you,' he said, handing back the passes to Jo. 'The petty officer will now escort you to the main gate.'

'Oh no he won't,' countered the Doctor. 'I was asking you a question. Do those stars indicate where the three ships sank?'

'As a matter of fact,' said Captain Hart, 'yes.'

The Doctor inspected the wall chart more carefully. 'So all the trouble is centred around this one particular oil-rig. The sooner I get out there, the better.' He turned back to Captain Hart. 'Do you think some of your fellows could run me over there?'

'Certainly not!' stormed Captain Hart. 'If you people from UNIT want to go joy-riding, you can fix up your own transport!'

'As a matter of fact,' said the Doctor, 'we have.' He turned to Jo. 'Come along, my dear.' He turned back to the captain. 'You won't mind if I leave by the same unconventional means that I arrived—towards the sea?'

'How you leave this establishment,' said Captain Hart, 'is no concern of mine, as long as you leave. UNIT doesn't run this country, you know. If any more of your people want to come here, perhaps they'd be good enough to ask permission!'

'I'm sure you're right,' said the Doctor, and ushered Jo out.

The petty officer kept close to them as they went down the stairs of the administrative block and back to the concrete roadway that ran outside.

'Want to get back to your boat?' asked the petty officer.

'Thank you,' said the Doctor, and allowed himself and Jo to be escorted back to the fishing-boat. The petty officer remained on the quayside, watching them carefully, until they were well out to sea.

. . . . .

Warm and comfortable in his luxurious basement 'cell', the Master was watching television when Trenchard arrived with the charts.

'Here we are, old man,' said Trenchard, setting down on a table the huge rolled-up charts. 'I think I've got everything you asked for.'

The Master switched off his television set, and unrolled one of the charts. It was identical to the one that the Doctor had seen on the wall of Captain Hart's office, showing the island and mainland, and the contours of the sea-bed.

'Excellent,' said the Master. 'You know, Trenchard, a man of your efficiency is wasted in a job like this—governor of a prison with only one prisoner!'

Trenchard was delighted by the Master's compliment. 'Well, I suppose it's a bit of a come-down. I was once the governor of a colony, you know.'

'Yes, yes, so I heard,' said the Master as he studied the chart. 'Never mind. When our plan succeeds everyone will recognise your true worth.' Then he drew lines on the chart using a ruler; the lines connected the three points of the recent sinkings.

Trenchard was curious. 'What are you doing?'

'These are the three points of the sinkings,' said the Master. 'And here in the centre is an oil-rig.'

'By jove,' exclaimed Trenchard, 'you're right. In fact, that's the one they closed down because they had so much trouble there. One of these oil men was telling me about it in the local pub. It's being overhauled now, and they've just left a couple of fellows there to act as caretakers.'

The Master straightened up. 'We must get sonar equipment and search that whole area!'

'Sonar equipment?' queried Trenchard.

'Electronic equipment to probe the sea-bed,' explained the Master.

'I know what sonar equipment is,' said Trenchard, 'but where do we get any from?'

'It's obvious,' said the Master. He pointed to a place on the map not far from the château itself. 'The Naval base. Use your influence.'

'It's out of the question,' Trenchard protested. 'They'd never agree to that.'

'Then we must steal it,' said the Master.

'Steady on, old man,' said Trenchard, desperately trying to remember that he was supposed to be the prison

42

governor and that the Master was his prisoner. 'I can't go along with that sort of behaviour. You're asking me to commit a criminal act!'

'If I had my freedom,' said the Master, 'that's what I'd do.'

Trenchard was silent, torn between his loyalty to the Prison Department who had appointed him to this job, and the plan that he had agreed with the Master.

The Master realised he may have gone too far with Trenchard. He said, 'You are, of course, right, Trenchard, in refusing to commit a crime. But the deliberate sinking of three ships, and the murder of all hands on board, was a far worse criminal act.'

'It was disgraceful,' said Trenchard with feeling, and glad to have something he could agree with.

'The question is,' said the Master, 'how many more lives will be lost? Isn't it your duty to save those lives, and to defeat the enemies of your country?'

Trenchard thought about this. Of one thing he was absolutely sure—the sinking of three ships, in mysterious circumstances, all in the same area, could not be a coincidence. Through conversations with the Master, whose intelligence he had come to respect, he now firmly believed that these sinkings were being caused by experiments with some new and terrible form of underwater weapon. The only question that remained was—who was doing it? As a keen follower of international political news, he knew that since World War Two the Soviet Union had been steadily building up the biggest navy the world had ever seen, and that this consisted largely of submarines.

'Apart from committing a criminal act,' said Trenchard, 'there is no practical way to acquire naval sonar equipment without their knowledge. That Naval base is a top security establishment. There are guards everywhere. Do you propose that I should jump over the barbed wire and dodge the sentries?'

'Nothing so dramatic as that,' said the Master. 'We shall drive in through the front gate . . .'

43

4

Stranded!

The Doctor manœuvred the little boat alongside the ladder that ran down one leg of the oil-rig. A stiff wind was blowing up a heavy swell. The Doctor managed to make up the boat's line to the ladder, then helped Jo to scramble across to it.

'I still say you should have taken Mr Robbins' boat back,' Jo called, as she climbed the vertical ladder.

'I will, Jo,' called the Doctor, now beneath her and climbing. 'And you can return his bicycle at the same time, poor man.'

Jo found it heavy going climbing up to the top. As she ascended, she took care not to look down in case it made her feel dizzy. She was much relieved when finally she pulled herself up on to the enclosed deck of the oil-rig. She found herself in a long wide passage that ran the length of one side of the rig. The metal wall on the outer side had big windows at regular intervals, the glass containing wire mesh to stop them from cracking in a heavy storm. With the metal deck and metal walls it was like the interior of a ship, except that there was no roll.

The Doctor pulled himself on to the deck. 'It's not what you'd describe as teeming with life,' observed the Doctor, looking up and down the passage.

'Maybe they're not working here today,' said Jo.

'You don't think they just come out here to work, do you?' said the Doctor. 'Men live on these things for weeks at a time. Let's take a look around.'

They went along the corridor and found that there were more leading off to other parts of the rig, and steps that led up to another deck above. After fifteen minutes of searching they found a cabin that was, or had been, inhabited. It was fitted out with bunks, a table and chairs, a small cooking-stove in a corner, and men's clothes were lying around. On the table was a game of draughts, which the players had obviously left in the middle, and half a glass of beer.

'Just like the *Marie Celeste*,' commented the Doctor.

'What's that?' Jo asked.

'A ship that was once found at sea,' the Doctor explained. 'There was food on the table, and all the other signs of life, but no one on board. All the passengers and crew had vanished without trace, and were never seen again.'

Jo shivered. 'Couldn't you be a bit more cheerful? This rig is huge. The men could be anywhere.'

'Why didn't they finish their game of draughts before they went off to do whatever they had to do?' said the Doctor.

Jo was beginning to feel uneasy. 'I've no idea,' she snapped. 'Let's just find them, and stop thinking of nasty ideas!' She glanced out of the porthole set in the wall of the cabin. 'And another thing, Doctor. It's beginning to get dark. We ought to get back to the island.'

'There's plenty of time,' said the Doctor. 'Even if we go back in the dark, there must be lights on at the Naval base or at the café—I can just point the boat towards the shore lights—'

He stopped suddenly as they both heard a loud explosion. Jo rushed to the porthole and looked down. 'Our boat,' she cried. 'Look!'

The Doctor joined Jo at the porthole. From here they could see straight down into the water a hundred feet below. A few pieces of broken, charred wood were floating at the bottom of the ladder—all that remained of Mr. Robbins' boat.

'It must have been the petrol tank,' said the Doctor.

'Petrol tanks can't blow up by themselves,' said Jo. 'Do you realise we're stranded here?'

'Not to worry,' said the Doctor. 'There must be a radio on this rig. I'll send a message back to shore. But it's a pity about that man's boat.'

Jo put her fingers to his lips. 'Shhh!'

The Doctor listened and heard nothing. 'What is it?'

Jo pointed to the deck-head. 'There's somebody moving about up there.'

'I shouldn't wonder, after that explosion. Probably everybody on board is craning their necks to see what happened,' said the Doctor. 'Let's go and find them all.'

The Doctor left the cabin, Jo following. Out in the passage the Doctor started to call out 'Hello? Anyone around?' There was no answer.

'It was above somewhere,' said Jo as they neared a metal staircase leading upwards.

The Doctor bounded up the stairs. 'Hello? Anyone at home?'

Now they were on another deck. They stopped and listened, but there was no sound of any living thing.

'I definitely heard someone moving up here,' Jo said.

'We can but search,' said the Doctor, and moved off down one of the many corridors leading from the deck.

Jo thought to follow, then realised it would save time if she did a little searching on her own. She went to the opening of another corridor, and stood stock still. 'Doctor,' she called, 'quick!'

The Doctor came running to her side. 'What is it?'

Jo pointed down the corridor. 'I think it's a man.'

The light was failing fast, and all they could see at the far end of the corridor was a huddled mound on the deck. The Doctor led the way to the end of the passage. It was indeed a man, doubled up and lying very still. His rough denim trousers and heavy roll-neck sweater suggested that he worked on the rig. The Doctor bent down close to the man and touched him. Then he straightened up.

'Poor chap. He's dead.' The Doctor moved round so that he could see the face of the corpse. 'I don't see any obvious marks. He might just have had a heart attack.'

Jo knew the Doctor was only saying this to put her at ease. 'He's been killed,' she said. 'I think it's time we

46

found a radio, if there is one, and got someone out here to us.'

'Perhaps you're right,' said the Doctor. 'Also this poor fellow's people will have to be told the sad news.'

They moved back down to the main deck. Just as they came to the bottom of the stairway, they both stopped dead. There was no mistaking the sound of dragging footsteps coming along one of the corridors that opened on to the deck. The Doctor looked round quickly, and drew Jo into the opening of one of the passage-ways. 'I suggest,' he said, 'that we keep absolutely still.'

The dragging footsteps came closer. Then, from their hiding place, they saw a man emerge from one of the corridors. He was a big fresh-faced man, wearing grubby blue jeans and a heavy sweater. Clutched firmly in his giant-sized hand was an evil-looking monkey-wrench.

'Just an ordinary *homo sapiens*,' whispered the Doctor. 'Let's be grateful that it was nothing more terrifying.' He stepped out on to the deck where the man could see him. 'Hello!'

The man stopped and turned. He was breathing very heavily, like someone in a state of severe fright. On seeing the Doctor his eyes dilated and he rocked on his heels.

'I know we're trespassing,' said the Doctor pleasantly, 'but we wanted to find out a few things.'

Suddenly, the man raised the monkey-wrench and charged straight at the Doctor. The Doctor sidestepped, then tripped the man as he went by. He fell heavily on to the metal deck, the monkey-wrench spinning from his hand. Before the man had time to struggle to his feet, the Doctor had sprung upon him and was applying a Venusian judo hold. The man was not in pain, but he was as helpless as a child where he lay.

'It's all right, old man,' said the Doctor. 'We don't mean to harm you.'

The man looked up into the Doctor's face, his eyes wild with fear. 'Hickman,' he said, his breathing becoming heavier, 'he's dead. It killed him.'

'What killed him?' asked the Doctor.

'Lizard,' said the man. 'Tall as a man—taller!' Then he collapsed into a faint. The Doctor relinquished his hold on his captive.

Jo stepped out from the opening to the corridor. 'Is he dead?'

'No,' said the Doctor. 'But he's a bit deranged. I'd better get him to that cabin we found.' Despite the man's size and weight, the Doctor was able to yank him up on to his back and carry him. 'You lead the way, Jo.'

Jo obeyed because the Doctor was almost bent double under the man's weight and couldn't see where he was going. She managed to find the inhabited cabin again and the Doctor laid his burden down on to one of the bunks.

'This man is suffering from severe shock,' pronounced the Doctor after he had carried out an inspection of the man. 'We must get him to a hospital.'

'With no boat,' Jo asked, 'how do we get him anywhere?'

The man on the bunk started to murmur something. The Doctor spoke quietly and calmly to him. 'You're safe now, old chap. Where is your radio transmitter?'

The man pointed to a cupboard. While the Doctor crossed to the cupboard containing the transmitter, Jo tried to talk to the man.

'What's your name?' she asked.

'Clark,' he muttered. 'Alan Clark . . .' His eyes rolled wildly. 'Lizards,' he said, choking on the word. 'Man-sized lizards. They killed Hickman . . . Sea-Devils . . .'

Jo spun round to the Doctor. 'He's talking about lizards again.'

But the Doctor was preoccupied staring at a mass of torn wires and smashed radio apparatus in the cupboard. 'I'm afraid some unwelcome visitors have been here before us,' he said. He came back to the side of the bunk. 'Tell me, old chap, do any of the crew have transistorised receiving units?'

Clark looked up, not understanding. 'Have what?'

Jo said, 'Trannies. Do any of you have a tranny?'

'Yeah,' said Clark. 'In the lockers . . . down the next corridor . . . you might find one.'

'What do you intend to do?' Jo asked the Doctor. 'Listen to *Pick of the Pops*?'

'It's possible to turn a receiver into a transmitter,' he explained '. . . simply a matter of modulating the signal. You connect the output of the loudspeaker into the input of the low frequency amplifier. Then you connect the output of your low frequency amplifier to your oscillator. Use your loudspeaker as a microphone, and there you are. Do you get the idea?'

Jo nodded. 'As long as you don't ask me to repeat it.'

The Doctor moved to the door. 'See if you can make him a cup of tea or something, with plenty of sugar.'

The Doctor stepped out into the corridor. Clark had said 'down the next corridor', so the Doctor went along to the main deck and found the opening to another passage-way. There was almost no lighting here, and he had to grope his way along to find the various doors opening into different cabins. On opening the first door he was hit by three brooms and a mop which fell out at him. He passed on quickly to the next door, turned the handle, gently pushed it ajar, and by groping found a light switch. The cabin contained two rows of tall metal lockers. Some were locked, but others containing the personal possessions of more trusting oil men were unlocked. He quickly sorted his way through piles of thick greasy sweaters, sea boots, used and unused underwear, to find what he wanted. Within a few minutes he had half-a-dozen pocket transistor radios safely in his enormous pockets. He turned off the light and started to go back towards the deck down the corridor. Framed in the opening of the entrance on to the main deck was the huge form of a Sea-Devil.

With the deck lights behind it, the Doctor could not see the Sea-Devil's face, but from its shape he knew what he had encountered. He stood very still. 'Don't be afraid,' he said. 'I don't wish to harm you.'

The Sea-Devil, who was equally surprised by the

49

A sudden beam of intense heat was emitted from the Sea-Devil's weapon.

sudden encounter, now raised its right hand. A sudden beam of intense heat was emitted from the weapon carried in the Devil's right hand. It struck the metal wall close to the Doctor's head, instantly turning the cold metal into white hot liquid.

The Doctor turned and fled for his life down the corridor. At its far end it led out on to the enclosed upper deck on the other side of the rig. He ran along this, then turned into the parallel corridor. Within moments he was back in the cabin with Jo and Alan Clark. Jo was boiling a kettle.

'How about a cup of tea?' she asked, before registering the Doctor's state of urgency.

'Just met a Sea-Devil,' he said. 'A related species to those lizard men we met in the caves in Derbyshire.[1] Completely hostile!'

As he talked he was shutting and bolting the door. Then he took the main electrical lead to the smashed radio transmitter and connected both its terminals to the metal bulkhead.

'What are you going to do?' Jo said.

'They can cut through rock, metal, anything,' said the Doctor. 'This is one way we may be able to fight back.'

Even as he spoke a circle of heat started to appear in the thick metal panel of the door, as though an oxyacetyline burner was being played on it from the outside. The circle of heat was exactly the same diameter as the circular marks on the underside of the lifeboat now held at the Naval base. Within a few seconds a round disc of metal had fallen out of the door. The Sea-Devil's scaly hand came in through the hole, groping for the bolts. The Doctor switched on the electric power that would normally feed the radio transmitter. There was a flash of electricity across the hole in the door, and a roar of pain from the Sea-Devil as it whipped its hand back through the aperture.

'Quick,' ordered the Doctor, 'help me unbolt the door.'

[1] See DOCTOR WHO AND THE CAVE MONSTERS

'What are you going to do?' asked Jo anxiously.

'Go after it, of course,' said the Doctor, feverishly pulling back the bolts with Jo's help.

They went out into the corridor and listened. From the distance they could hear the groans of the Sea-Devil, still shocked from the charge of high voltage electricity.

'This way, I think,' said the Doctor, and went off down the corridor.

Jo followed cautiously. 'It could be leading us into a trap,' she said. 'There may be others of them.'

The Doctor had already reached the main deck. 'Look,' he said, pointing down the deck. It was almost dark now, but Jo could see the silhouette of the Sea-Devil as it lurched along the deck. Then it reeled towards one of the wire-meshed windows, and fell straight through it—and was gone. A couple of seconds later they heard the splash as the Sea-Devil hit the surface of the sea.

'You realise,' Jo said quietly, 'that if it isn't dead, it will return here with all its friends?'

'But we've found how to defend ourselves,' said the Doctor.

'I asked Mr. Clark where the electricity comes from for this rig,' Jo said. 'There's a cable on the sea-bed that comes from the mainland. If the Sea-Devils cut that, we've got no light or heat—and no means of defence.'

'Then let us hope,' said the Doctor, 'that the thought doesn't occur to them. Did you say something about a cup of tea?' They turned and went back down the corridor towards the inhabited cabin.

5

Air-Sea Rescue

Police-constable Watkins stood before Captain Hart's desk, his helmet respectfully held beneath his arm. 'You say he called here, sir?'

Captain Hart nodded. 'Late yesterday afternoon. Then a young lady turned up with UNIT passes for both of them.'

'And he arrived by boat?' said P.C. Watkins. It was the first time he had ever been inside the Naval Base, and he intended to make the most of it. For fifteen years he had been the only policeman on the island, where he knew everyone and everybody's business, and it rankled with him that this Naval Base was virtually out-of-bounds to him. Today, however, he had a perfect right to be here. He was investigating what, by the values of the island and its tiny population, was Big Time Crime —someone had stolen Thomas Robbins's boat.

'I think we are repeating ourselves,' said Captain Hart, who wanted to get on with his own job. New sonar equipment was due to arrive at any moment, and he would have to be present to check it over. 'He arrived in a boat, somewhat unexpectedly, and then this young lady turned up.'

'And they both left in the boat?' said Watkins.

'Yes,' replied Hart for about the third time. 'They left in his boat.'

'Well it wasn't his,' said Watkins. 'He's stolen that boat from one of the fishermen, and he hasn't returned it yet. Did he tell you where he was going off to?'

Captain Hart tried to remember. A lot of things had happened in his busy life since yesterday afternoon. 'He wanted to visit an oil-rig—this one,' and he rose from behind his desk and indicated the rig on his wall chart.

'What did he want to go there for?' asked P.C. Watkins.

Hart gave thought to this. He firmly believed that the Doctor was mentally unbalanced, or at least eccentric; but he was connected with UNIT, and possibly everything that was discussed yesterday should be regarded as secret. 'I've no idea,' Hart lied.

P.C. Watkins had not been a policeman all his life without recognising a lie when it was told to him. 'Come now, sir,' he said, 'surely if he told you that he wanted to go to the oil-rig, he must have said why?'

Hart was now distinctly annoyed with Watkins, because clearly the latter realised he had lied. But having told the lie, he now had to defend it. 'He was a very eccentric gentleman. I'm afraid that I can say no more than that.'

Watkins closed his notebook. He, Watkins, was now distinctly annoyed with Captain Hart, because Captain Hart was excluding him from something that was going on. Watkins liked to be the trusted servant, and not to be treated as a child. 'Very well, sir,' he said. 'I shall have to report this to my superiors.' It contained just the hint of a threat.

'Report it to whomsoever you like,' said Captain Hart carelessly. 'I must now get on with my work.'

Watkins replaced his helmet on his head *before* leaving Hart's office, just to remind the captain that he represented the Law.

Alone, Captain Hart spent a few moments thinking over what P.C. Watkins had told him. Although a bit odd in his way of doing things, clearly the Doctor was not the sort of person who would *steal* a man's boat, or even borrow it without taking it back. The oil-rig was not very far from the island, and although there had been a heavy swell late yesterday afternoon, at no time had the sea been particularly rough. On that basis, the trip to the oil-rig and back would have been well within the range of the little boat in which Hart had seen the Doctor arrive at the base yesterday. So what had happened to the man? Why would he voluntarily stay on the oil-rig all night?

With these thoughts in mind Captain Hart got up and went into the next office, the Naval Base's radio-room. Leading Telegraphist Bryson was on duty.

'Bryson,' said Hart, 'whistle up oil-rig No. 5, will you?'

'Anything in particular, sir?' asked Bryson, as he adjusted his transmitter to the oil-rig's wavelength.

'I don't know,' said Hart. 'Let's see if we can get an answer first.'

Bryson spoke into a microphone: '*HMS Foxglove calling oil-rig five. I repeat, HMS Foxglove calling oil-rig five.*' As with all Naval shore-establishments, the base had a name like a ship, and the name was always preceded with the words HMS—Her Majesty's Ship.

'How long do they usually take to reply?' asked Hart.

'When they're fully operational, sir,' said Bryson, 'there's always a sparks on duty. But No. 5's only got two maintenance men on her. You know, that's the rig where everything kept breaking down.'

'Yes,' said Captain Hart thoughtfully, 'I remember.' He suddenly made up his mind what had to be done. 'Forget the call Bryson, and call up air-sea rescue.'

.   .   .   .

Jo opened a tin of baked beans and poured the contents into a little saucepan. They had had beans for breakfast, and now they would have to have beans for lunch. She could not find any other food anywhere on the oil-rig. Clark was at last sleeping peacefully, having had a troubled night full of bad dreams, and the Doctor was engrossed with building a complicated radio transmitter circuit from what remained of half-a-dozen pocket radios. Jo looked across at him and the tangle of wires strewn all over the table.

'How's it going?' she asked.

'Nearly finished,' he said. 'I'm just about to test it.' He made a few final adjustments. 'Now,' he said proudly, 'let's see if we can call up the outside world!'

The Doctor turned on a switch that he had introduced into the circuits. From six tiny loudspeakers they heard one of the familiar voices of BBC Radio 1 : '*—and here's a question for all serious motorists. If your car breaks down between Trafalgar Square and Aldwych, are you Stranded? Oh well, can't win 'em all, so let's move on to another golden oldie by the Beatles—*' The

55

Doctor turned off the switch, rested his chin on his hands and studied the mass of wires. 'Somehow I must have forgotten to reverse the circuits,' he muttered.

'Maybe some food will help you to think better,' suggested Jo. 'It'll be ready soon.' She got on with cooking the beans while the Doctor set to work again with his wires, diodes and transistors.

After a few moments had passed Jo said, 'Last night . . . that thing that attacked us . . . you said it was related to something that came out of caves in Derbyshire?'

'That's right,' said the Doctor, as though that closed the matter.

'Well,' she said, 'can you explain what you meant?'

'It's a rather sad story,' the Doctor began.[1] 'You see, millions of years ago reptiles were the masters of this planet.'

'I know all about the dinosaurs,' said Jo.

'*Everybody* knows about the dinosaurs,' said the Doctor, rather resenting the interruption. 'What people don't know is that the reptiles also developed a highly intelligent form of humanoid, *homo reptilia*. These creatures believed that Earth was going to be badly affected by the arrival of a rogue planet from outer space, so they prepared deep underground shelters for themselves. The little planet didn't cause any great harm at all—in fact, it got caught within Earth's gravity and went into orbit around it.'

'The Moon!' exclaimed Jo.

'Exactly,' said the Doctor. 'These reptile men and women had put themselves into deep hibernation, so that they wouldn't use up any food or oxygen while they were in their shelters. Their plan was that special triggers on the surface would re-activate them all once the little planet had gone on its way. But because it went into orbit instead, and became the Moon, the triggering mechanisms never worked.'

Jo asked, 'How many of these shelters did they build?'

[1] See DOCTOR WHO AND THE CAVE MONSTERS

'I've no idea,' said the Doctor. 'Possibly thousands, all over the world. When the reptile men started to be re-activated up in Derbyshire, you can imagine how they felt about *homo sapiens* being the masters now.'

'I don't know that I can,' said Jo.

The Doctor paused in his work to make his point. 'Jo, if you went to sleep for, say, twenty years in your home, and then woke up to find it had been taken over by rats and mice, how would you feel about that?'

'I'd want to clear them out,' Jo said. 'I see what you mean now. These reptiles think of humans as vermin?'

'Naturally,' said the Doctor. 'To them, Earth is *their* planet, and always has been. As far as they're concerned, Man is an ape who's risen above himself.'

'If they'd been hibernating for millions of years,' Jo asked, 'what woke them up?'

'In Derbyshire it was the presence of a cyclotrone us-ing enormous amounts of electrical power,' said the Doctor. 'Here, for this is clearly what we're witnessing again, I don't know . . . probably something to do with the drilling being carried out by this oil-rig.' He sat back and regarded his make-do radio transmitter. 'I think that should work now. What's our call sign?'

Jo left her stove to look around the smashed-up trans-mitter. 'It's written on the wall here,' she said, 'ZXT 413.'

The Doctor switched on, then picked up one of the pocket transistors and spoke into its loudspeaker: '*May Day . . . May Day . . . This is ZXT 413. We are stranded on the oil-rig. Please send immediate assistance. Can you hear me? Can you hear me? Over.*' The Doctor turned on the pocket radio that he had left intact as a receiver, although he had altered its wavebands down to ultra-short-wave.

'What's May Day got to do with it?' Jo asked.

'French for "aid me",' replied the Doctor. 'Look,' and he scribbled it down on a piece of paper so that Jo would understand. *M'aidez.* 'It's used internationally nowa-days,' he added, 'instead of SOS.'

'No one's answering,' said Jo.

'Have patience, my dear, we shouldn't expect miracles—'

His words were overspoken by a strong masculine voice coming from the one receiving pocket radio: *'Hello, oil-rig. Hello, oil-rig. Have received you loud and clear. Am about to land.'*

Even as the voice spoke they heard the roar of a helicopter directly overhead.

'You say we shouldn't expect miracles?' said Jo, with a grin. 'What do you call *that*?'

.   .   .   .

While the Doctor, Jo, and Clark were being lifted off the oil-rig in the air-sea rescue Naval helicopter that had been sent out by Captain Hart long before the Doctor had managed to transmit his May Day message, George Trenchard was slowly driving his landrover along the approach leading to the château. He drove slowly because he wanted time to think, and he wanted to think because he was about to commit a crime.

Trenchard had been immediately impressed by the intelligence of the Master, his one charge, and by the man's seeming desire to become a reformed character. Even so, he was wary: it would not be the first time a prisoner had pretended to become reformed in order that security should be relaxed, thus allowing him to escape. Trenchard had heard all about *those* tricks. And then these ships started disappearing, and it was the Master who had produced the only possible explanation for them: some unknown enemies of England were trying out some deadly new weapon, just off the coast. Trenchard was in favour of relaying this information directly to the Government, but the Master pointed out that in a situation as dangerous as this no one could be trusted. What they needed was proof. In any case, the Master had said, if the Government was informed at this stage, someone else would be bound to get the credit. The Master's plan was that he and Trenchard would work together to get to the root of the problem; then Trenchard would truly qualify for the recognition he so richly deserved, while the Master would remain quietly in the background.

Already Trenchard could see himself receiving a knighthood for his services to England in detecting and exposing its enemies.

Yet there remained in Trenchard's mind the lurking suspicion that the Master was going to trick him. This thought haunted him as he halted the landrover outside the front door of the château. He reached behind his driving seat and brought out a large cardboard box, carefully carried it under his arm and gave his own coded knock on the front door. The door was opened immediately by the prison officer on duty. A minute later Trenchard was entering the Master's basement room. The Master regarded the cardboard box with obvious pleasure.

'No problems?' asked the Master.

Trenchard waited until the prison officer had closed the door and they were alone. 'It isn't easy getting this sort of thing at a moment's notice. Had to go over to the mainland to get it, of course. The blighter in the shop knew who I was.'

'What did you say?'

'Had to make up a story,' said Trenchard, 'said we were going to have some theatricals here.'

'How very ingenious,' said the Master, always quick to compliment Trenchard. 'May I see?'

Trenchard stepped back from the box. 'Help yourself. Hope it all fits.'

As the Master opened the box, Trenchard felt that he had to say what was uppermost in his mind. 'You realise I'm committing a crime doing this, old man?'

'Mr. Trenchard,' said the Master, turning to him. 'I am only too aware of the risk you are taking. That is why I don't intend to let you down.'

'Just as long as we understand each other,' remarked Trenchard. 'Aren't you going to try it on?'

'Of course,' said the Master. He lifted one of the items out of the box, a Naval officer's cap, and put it on. 'How do I look?'

.   .   .   .

Captain Hart had listened with as much patience as possible to the Doctor's incredible story. He hardly believed a word of it. When the Doctor had finished, Hart got up from his desk and walked over to the window overlooking the Naval Base. It was his favourite place for thinking. Then he turned to the Doctor and Jo.

'How do you really expect me to believe in . . . in Sea-Devils?' he asked.

'We *both* saw one,' said Jo.

'Now just a minute,' said Captain Hart, sensing an inconsistency, 'a little while ago you said you only saw a silhouette, Miss Grant.'

'It was the silhouette of a Sea-Devil,' insisted Jo, exasperated by the captain's disbelief. 'In any case, you've spoken to the man we brought back from the oil-rig. *He* saw one kill his friend.'

That was true. On their return in the helicopter, Clark had been put straight into the sick-bay, and Captain Hart had spoken to him there. Even so, Hart remained sceptical. But he tried to be fair. 'I want to put this suggestion to you both,' he said. 'The man Clark is obviously in a very poorly condition—mentally, I mean. Let us presume that yesterday, for some reason, he killed his companion—'

The Doctor suddenly interjected: 'You're accusing that man of murder!'

'I'm simply suggesting what *might* have happened,' said Captain Hart, and then continued: 'While mentally unbalanced, he killed his companion. Then you two arrived. As you pointed out, Doctor, he tried to kill you. Fortunately, he was unsuccessful in that attempt, but he *may* have been successful in communicating his madness to you.'

'Captain Hart,' said the Doctor with studied emphasis, 'I know about communicated madness. I can assure you that none of us are mad. I have seen, and been chased by, a Sea-Devil.'

Captain Hart came back and sat down again at his desk. He was an intelligent man, but he was being asked to believe in something which exceeded all his previous knowledge. 'All right,' he said at last. 'May I, for the sake of my own conscience, hear your story again?'

Jo got angry. 'We've already told you everything!'

'It's all right, Jo,' said the Doctor. 'Captain Hart's quite right in wanting to be sure that we are telling the truth.' Slowly, and carefully, the Doctor started to tell Captain Hart once more about the events on the oil-rig.

. . . . .

Trenchard drove his landrover carefully along the road leading to the Naval Base. From time to time he glanced at the heap of rugs, travelling blankets, and his golf bags, which made a mound on the floor behind his driving seat. He had already committed one major crime—allowing his prisoner to leave the prison without authority from the Prison Department. Now, as he approached the gates of the Naval Base, he was about to commit yet another— he was going to delude a representative of the Lords of the Admiralty into believing that he, Trenchard, was the only occupant of the landrover.

At the gates he stopped, and their Lordships' representative, in the person of Chief Petty Officer Beaver, came up to the driver's window and saluted. ' 'Afternoon, Mr. Trenchard. Want to see the captain?'

'If I may,' said Trenchard, always polite to lower-deck ratings. 'I was just passing.'

'I think he's got visitors,' said C.P.O. Beaver, 'but I imagine he'll have time for you.' He opened the gates to admit the landrover. As Trenchard went by he called out cheerfully, 'How's the Master getting on?'

Trenchard almost jumped out of his driving seat. 'Very

well, thank you,' he said, 'considering . . .' He realised Beaver's question had no point behind it; it was just a pleasantry. After all, everyone on the island knew about the château and its celebrated prisoner.

Usually when Trenchard visited Captain Hart he parked his landrover right outside the main administrative block. It was his little way of showing that he was a cut above the other people who parked in the base's car-park. Today, however, he decided it was wise to follow the custom of the common herd. He headed his landrover into the car-park at the side of the main building, and stationed it unobtrusively between two other vehicles. He stopped the motor, carefully pocketed the keys, and noted that his heart seemed to be pounding very fast. Without looking round to the mound of rugs and blankets behind him he said, 'We are now in the car-park. I shall be gone for about twenty minutes.' There was no reply.

Trenchard slowly got out of the landrover. His legs felt unsteady, as though his knees had turned to soapy water. Then he tried to remember that he was, first and foremost, a soldier, and soldiers must be brave. He knew, or hoped he knew, that what he was doing was right. He was trying to save England from her enemies. The difficult thing about it, though, was that in order to do the right thing he had to do so many *wrong* things. He was a very, very worried man as he walked, a little unsteadily, from the car-park in the direction of the administrative building.

Once Trenchard's footsteps had gone out of earshot, the heap of rugs and blankets started to move, and the Master cautiously reared his head. There was no one about, so he climbed out of the landrover and paused to brush down his smart-looking Naval officer's uniform. Amused, he looked at the bands on his cuffs—the theatrical costumiers had made him into a commander, which was pretty high-ranking. He straightened his cap, and marched across the car-park, returning the salutes of two passing lower-deck ratings.

Captain Hart had now heard the Doctor's story for the second time. He said nothing for a while because he wanted to give his mind time to consider the idea of intelligent beings living somewhere on, or under, the sea-bed. Finally, he looked up. 'Let us say, Doctor, that I accept your theory about the existence of these Sea-Devils. What would you want me to do?'

The Doctor was emphatic. 'We must devise some means to make contact with them!'

'Whatever for?!' exclaimed Captain Hart. 'These things are sinking ships.'

'These things, as you call them,' said the Doctor, 'are an intelligent form of life. I've already explained that they used to be the masters of this planet—'

There was a knock on the door, and W.R.N. Writer Jane Blythe looked in. 'Excuse me, sir. Mr. Trenchard would like a word with you.'

Hart looked up. 'Didn't you tell him I was busy?'

'He said he'd only be a moment, sir.' Jane lowered her voice to a whisper. 'He's just outside, behind me.'

Captain Hart tried to put a good face on it. 'All right. Wheel him in.'

Jane stepped to one side, and ushered in Trenchard. He advanced on Hart with outstretched hand. 'Got a minute, old chap? Just wanted to talk to you about the golf tournament—' He stopped as he saw the Doctor and Jo. 'I'll be blowed! I thought you two left the island yesterday.'

'We got delayed,' said Jo.

'Taking a look round the island, eh? Charming place, what there is of it.' Trenchard returned his attention to Captain Hart. 'Look, John, I don't want to butt in, but about next weekend: we are rather relying on you to play, you know.'

'I'll do my best,' said Captain Hart. 'But if we happen to get a sudden flap on . . .' He left the rest of the sentence in mid-air.

'Then I'd better arrange to have a reserve standing by,' said Trenchard. 'What sort of player is that fellow Griffiths?'

The Doctor listened patiently while the two men discussed the relative pros and cons of various local golf players. He noticed how Hart seemed to be trying to get rid of Trenchard, whereas Trenchard was almost deliberately prolonging the conversation. It occurred to the Doctor that Trenchard seemed extremely nervous, and he wondered why.

.   .   .   .

While Trenchard played for time, the Master was busily helping himself to sonar spare parts in the Naval Base's store-room. It was a long hut containing rows of metal shelves. In this one place there was almost every electronic spare part he would ever need for the apparatus that he intended to construct back in his room at the château. By good luck he had found a small duffel bag in a corner of the store-room, and he was carefully filling this when Chief Petty Officer Smedley happened to come in. Smedley was more than a little surprised at the spectacle of a commander who was literally getting his hands dirty.

'Excuse me, sir,' enquired C.P.O. Smedley, 'but should I know you?'

The Master, quite unperturbed, continued with his work. 'You most certainly should. Haven't you been informed that I was coming?'

'I'm afraid not, sir,' said Smedley.

'Special audit,' said the Master, stowing an expensive ohm-counter into the duffel bag, 'Ministry of Defence.' He looked further along the shelf and selected a low-voltage relay unit. He was about to put this into the bag when he paused, pretending only now to have noticed that the Chief Petty Officer was still standing there. 'Well, carry on, Chief.'

Smedley was very worried. Years of naval training had

taught him to respect officers without question, and this visitor was a very high-ranking officer indeed. But he just could not believe what he was watching. 'If I may be permitted to ask, sir,' he said, trembling slightly, and with visions of very shortly becoming an able seaman once more, 'may I see your pass?'

'Captain Hart's preparing it now,' said the Master. 'He'll be here with it in a moment.'

'Captain Hart is coming *here* with your pass, sir?' Smedley could not understand this at all. If a pass was to be sent, and that in itself was odd enough, the captain would have it sent by one of the ratings. 'If it is all the same to you, sir,' said Smedley, 'I shall have to double-check that, sir.' He had now shown enough insolence to a commissioned officer to lose him his chief's hooks, if not actually to have him confined to a naval prison. He turned to the wall telephone and lifted the handpiece.

The Master came up behind the C.P.O. 'Turn round,' he said in a firm, strong voice.

Smedley turned. 'Sir?'

'You will obey my orders, Chief Petty Officer,' said the Master, his piercing hypnotic eyes staring straight into those of Smedley's. 'Replace that telephone.'

Smedley slowly hung back the telephone handpiece, presenting his back to the Master. The Master's hand flashed as he delivered an almost fatal blow to the back of Smedley's neck. His victim fell heavily to the floor. The Master got back to his work of rifling the naval stores of all that he needed.

.   .   .   .   .

By now the Doctor had heard about the golfing abilities, and weaknesses, of a man called Spiecer, a retired Merchant Navy captain called Higgs, the island's vicar, the publican, and a financier who had his own yacht and wasn't very sociable. For a man who had said that his visit would only take a minute, George Trenchard had by now indulged himself with a full twenty-five minutes.

Always a gentleman, Captain Hart had at no time hinted he was in a hurry to get on with the discussion that Trenchard had interrupted. Completely bored with the two-handed conversation, Jo had gone and stationed herself at the office window where she could watch the seagulls. Now, at last, Trenchard seemed ready to leave.

'Now I don't want you to worry,' he was saying to Captain Hart. 'If you can't play in the tournament, we'll find someone else. Although, goodness knows, that isn't going to be easy.'

For a ghastly moment the Doctor thought Trenchard was going to recapitulate on *why* it wasn't going to be easy to replace Hart on the golf course. Perhaps Hart also feared that, for he quickly said, 'I haven't definitely said that I won't be there, George. Could we agree to cross that bridge when we come to it?'

'Of course,' said Trenchard. He looked at his watch. 'My goodness, I'd better be on my way. I realise how busy you are.' He moved to the door, which Jane Blythe quickly opened for him. But there he paused and turned to the Doctor. 'Staying on the island much longer?'

'That,' said the Doctor, 'depends on how long it takes me to conclude my business. Goodbye, Mr. Trenchard.'

'What? Oh, yes. I mustn't hold you up.' He turned to Jo at the window. 'Goodbye, Miss Grant. A great pleasure to see you again.'

Jo said goodbye from the window.

'Well,' said Trenchard, 'must be off.' And so, finally, he left them in peace.

Captain Hart smiled at the Doctor. The deadening personality of George Trenchard had formed a bond between them. 'You were saying, Doctor?' he said.

'I believe all shipping must be kept away from this area,' said the Doctor. 'That's for a start—'

But Hart raised his hand to stop the Doctor continuing. 'Doctor, these are major shipping lanes. In any case, you know what happens in the English Channel when there's a dangerous wreck. Half the foreign ships simply ignore the Trinity House marker buoys.'

'Then send ships out to patrol the area,' said the Doctor. 'Somehow ships must be kept away, to avoid further sinkings.'

Suddenly Jo let out a little shriek from her place at the window. 'Doctor! Quickly! Come here!'

The Doctor turned. 'I know this discussion may be boring you, Jo—'

'It's the Master,' she cut in, looking down at the concrete roadway below. 'Please come and look.'

The Doctor leapt over to the window and looked where Jo had pointed. 'Where is he?'

'You've missed him. He turned that corner.' Jo pointed now in the direction of the car-park, but from the window the car-park was not in sight.

From his desk Captain Hart asked: 'Do you two mind telling me what you're talking about?'

'A very dangerous criminal,' said the Doctor, 'loose in your base. I suggest you order a full security alert.'

'Doctor,' said the captain, with as much authority as he could muster, 'it is one thing when you tell me about intelligent reptiles destroying ships—' As he spoke the 'phone rang, and Jane Blythe quietly took the call— 'but when you start blabbering about dangerous criminals roaming about in this base, I start to question whether I should ever have listened to you at all!'

'Sir?' said Jane, putting down the 'phone.

Hart turned abruptly. 'What is it?'

'Chief Petty Officer Smedley, sir,' she said, '. . . he's been found knocked unconscious in the sonar supplies store.'

.   .   .   .   .

Trenchard drove his landrover slowly through the Naval Base towards the main gates. Before starting he had seen by the size and shape of the mounds of rugs and blankets in the back that the Master was already on board. Chief Petty Officer Beaver was still on duty at the gates, and opened them immediately he saw the familiar landrover. To Trenchard's surprise, however, as the landrover neared the open gate C.P.O Beaver raised his hand for Trenchard to stop. He came round to the driving window.

'Anything wrong?' enquired Trenchard, trying to conceal the terror in his mind.

'I think there may be, sir,' said the Chief. He leant right inside the cabin, and looked at the mound of rugs and blankets. 'Collecting for a jumble sale, sir?'

Trenchard tried to keep his nerve. He smiled, rather weakly. 'No. Just a few odds and ends. Ought to clean out this old bus sometime.' He licked his parched lips. 'You say there may be something wrong, Chief Petty Officer?'

Beaver leant close to Trenchard's ear. 'The old chopper was out today, brought three people in from that there oil-rig. You know, the one where there's been all the trouble with the machinery and that.'

Trenchard sighed with relief. Beaver was a well-known gossip. 'Air-sea rescue, eh?'

The Chief nodded. 'Of course, they don't tell us anything. But one of the people they brought in was a girl. I didn't know they had girls on them oil-rigs.'

Trenchard put on a little laugh. 'Anything to keep the chaps out there happy, what?'

At this point alarm sirens started to wail from every corner of the base, and through his rear window Trenchard saw sailors wearing webbed gaiters falling in for emergency security stations, some of them with rifles. C.P.O. Beaver, however, took no notice.

'Well it's funny goings on if you ask me,' said the Chief.

'Yes, very funny,' said Trenchard, his foot poised on the accelerator to make a dash for it. 'Those sirens,' he asked, as if he did not know, 'do they mean something?'

The Chief looked up at the siren wailing loudly on top of his gatehouse. 'Emergency test of security, I suppose,' he concluded. 'Your pal Captain Hart likes to keep us on our toes. Anyway, you'd better be on your way, sir. By rights, the moment those sirens go I'm not supposed to let anyone ashore or on board.' (He used the Naval terms for going out and coming in.) 'So the sooner you're gone, I can get these gates closed up.'

'Right you are,' said Trenchard. 'Well, nice to have had a chat.'

Although desperate to get away at high speed, Trenchard drove his landrover in his usual slow manner. A lifetime as an army officer had taught him that he should always keep his nerve. As the landrover went away, Chief Petty Officer Beaver closed and locked the gates, then waved to Trenchard. Trenchard did not wave back.

.   .   .   .   .

The Doctor, Jo, and Captain Hart crowded round Chief Petty Officer Smedley's bunk in the sick-bay, the base's Medical Officer watching on.

'He was taking equipment, sir,' said Smedley, trying to lie to attention while addressing his commanding officer.

The Doctor asked, 'What did this officer look like?'

'About my height,' said Smedley. 'And he had a beard.'

'You see,' said Jo. 'The Master!'

Captain Hart signalled Jo to be careful what she said in front of the others. He turned to Smedley. 'All right, Chief. I'm sure you'll be better for a rest in the sick-bay.'

The captain walked away from the bunk, and gestured for the Doctor and Jo to follow. Out of earshot of Smedley, he turned to Jo. 'You referred to "the Master", both in my office and here. Are you talking about Mr. Trenchard's prisoner?'

'That's right,' said Jo. 'That's why we came to the island in the first place. To visit him.'

Captain Hart clearly wasn't convinced. 'But we all know about the security measures at the château,' he said. 'It's common gossip on the island. I saw the Master's pictures in the newspapers at the time of his trial, and I'm sure that any swarthy-looking fellow with a beard could be mistaken for the Master once he was dressed up in naval officers' uniform.'

'But I know his walk,' Jo protested. 'I'd know the Master anywhere.'

'I think,' said the Doctor, 'the question that's really perplexing Captain Hart is how the Master could be both a prisoner at the château, and raiding the sonar stores supplies here at the same time.' He turned to the captain. 'I'm afraid there's only one answer to that, Captain. Trenchard brought him here.'

With little conviction the captain said, 'George Trenchard is a personal friend of mine. I simply cannot believe it.'

The Doctor pressed his case. 'Mr. Trenchard arrived just before Chief Petty Officer Smedley found the man in the stores, and he left just a few moments ago. All that talk about who would play in the golf tournament, didn't it strike you as a little long-winded?'

Captain Hart smiled. 'Old Trenchard's always like that.' He paused to think. 'But I grant you, it was a bit odd the way he carried on and on today.'

'Personal friend or not,' said Jo, 'you ought to arrest that Mr. Trenchard straight away!'

'My dear Miss Grant,' said Captain Hart, 'that is quite out of the question. In the first place I have no authority to arrest anyone except inside this base. Secondly, we are condemning a man, who incidentally has served his country well for many years, on pure surmise. There isn't a shred of evidence against him.'

'Would you do one thing,' said the Doctor. 'Lend me some transport?'

'What do you want to do?' asked the Captain.

'Drive back to that château,' said the Doctor, 'and ask Mr. George Trenchard if his prisoner is missing.'

6

'This Man Came to Kill me!'

Trenchard was trying to calm his nerves by practising putting shots on the floor of his office. He had just been told over the internal telephone that the Doctor and Jo had arrived at the gatehouse in a naval jeep and wanted to see him. To have refused might have been suspicious, so he gave orders for them to be allowed into the grounds, provided they were accompanied from the gatehouse to the château by a prison officer.

He was just making a very tricky shot when there was a knock on the door and the two visitors were brought in. To test his nerves Trenchard made the shot before speaking. It missed by a good six inches.

'Hands a bit shaky?' enquired the Doctor wickedly.

'Out of practice,' said Trenchard, putting away his putting stick. 'Do you wish to visit the prisoner again?'

'That depends if he's still here,' said the Doctor. 'We have reason to believe that he's escaped.'

Trenchard sat down heavily behind his desk, his heart thumping very badly now. 'Escaped?' he echoed almost in a whisper. It was the only word that he could get out.

The Doctor smiled. 'You don't seem very surprised at the news.'

Trenchard tried to get his shattered mind in order. He should treat this a joke. It was the only thing he could do.

'I think you must be suffering from some mental aberration,' he said, touching his forehead, 'you know, a touch of the old berry-berry or something. Would you like to sit down and have a brandy?'

'I saw the Master with my own eyes at the Naval Base,' said Jo.

'Come now, Miss Grant,' said Trenchard, 'that's quite impossible.'

'A Chief Petty Officer caught the Master masquerading as a senior naval officer,' said the Doctor, 'stealing electronic equipment. The Master knocked the man out.'

Now Trenchard was really worried. The Master had said nothing to him about his encounter with a Chief Petty Officer. 'Well,' he said, 'I'd better look into this. Will you both wait here, please?'

Trenchard rose and went to the door.

Jo said, 'Why not use that monitor of yours?—see if he's still in his room?'

Trenchard hesitated, and tried to think of some reason for not doing the obvious. 'Don't really like gadgets,' he said. 'I want to see my prisoner with my own eyes.' He went out.

The Doctor immediately went to the 'phone on Trenchard's desk. As with all telephones in prisons, it had a little chain and padlock that immobilised the dial. He turned to Jo. 'Take the Jeep and get back to the Naval Base straight away. 'Phone UNIT—tell them that Trenchard and his entire staff must be arrested immediately!'

Jo said, 'What are you going to do?'

'Be a good guest,' said the Doctor, 'and twiddle my thumbs until Mr. Trenchard comes back.'

. . . .

Trenchard felt that he was making no impression on the Master at all. Here he was, telling the man that he'd been spotted when he was at the Naval Base, and the Master wasn't making any reaction at all. He seemed to be totally absorbed in drawing a diagram of electrical circuits, something quite beyond Trenchard's understanding.

'Will you listen to me?' said Trenchard, aware that he was going red in the face. 'They know *everything*!'

At last the Master turned away from his work. 'They *think* they know something, that's all,' he said. 'Why not

72

ask the Doctor to come down here and see me for himself?'

'Of course I can do that,' said Trenchard, 'but it won't make any difference. I wish you'd told me about that man you nearly killed. You shouldn't have kept that to yourself!'

'You'd only have panicked,' said the Master, which Trenchard knew was probably true. 'Send the Doctor down here and I'll tell him what we're doing.'

Trenchard was outraged. 'You mustn't! You said yourself it must be kept a secret until we can prove that what we are doing is right.'

'The Doctor is a very intelligent man, Mr. Trenchard,' said the Master. 'He'll understand, and he may be willing to help us.'

'And if he doesn't?' Trenchard asked.

The Master shrugged. 'People can only leave this place with your permission—Governor.' His voice acquired a rough hard edge: 'Now send him down here by himself. No prison officers present. Leave the rest to me. I'll win him over.'

Trenchard left to carry out the Master's order. All his time in the army had taught him that the simplest solution to any problem was to carry out an order given by someone else. Once Trenchard had gone, the Master quickly put away the diagram he was working on. Then, just to be on the safe side, he took a cushion and rammed it in the front of the television camera eye that continuously overlooked him. Satisfied that he could not be observed, he banged on the door. It was immediately opened by the prison officer on guard.

'Would you come in here a moment,' said the Master. 'I think something's wrong with the air-conditioning. There's no air coming in up there.' He pointed to one of the grilles near the ceiling.

The prison officer looked up towards the grille, taking his eyes off the Master for a moment. With a flashing karate chop, the Master knocked the officer unconscious and took his gun.

73

*With a flashing karate chop, the Master knocked the officer
unconscious . . .*

Trenchard came back into his office. He found the Doctor alone, reading the office copy of *HM Prison Regulations*. 'Where's Miss Grant?'

The Doctor closed the book. 'Gone back to the Naval Base. Got bored here. Did you find your prisoner?'

'Of course I did,' rejoined Trenchard. 'And now you're going to see him for yourself.' He called to the prison officer out in the hallway. 'Take this gentleman down to see the prisoner, then report back here immediately.'

'You're not coming along, too?' asked the Doctor.

'I have something rather urgent to do first,' said Trenchard. 'I'll see you later.'

The Doctor left with the prison officer. The moment the door was closed behind them, Trenchard lifted the internal 'phone to speak to the gatehouse. Under no circumstances was Miss Grant to be allowed to leave the grounds—at least not until the Master had convinced the Doctor that what he and Trenchard were doing was in the best interests of national security.

The Doctor and the prison officer arrived at the door to the Master's room.

'Why is there no officer outside the prisoner's door?' asked the Doctor.

'We do not discuss prison routines with visitors,' replied his escort, as though repeating something he had learnt from an instruction book.

The Doctor didn't press the matter. He waited while the officer put his key into the door's lock, turned it, and then pushed the door open. The officer stood back to let the Doctor enter. He closed the door.

The Master, who was sitting back, reading, exclaimed, 'My dear Doctor, two visits in two days. This is most touching.'

The Doctor got straight to the point. 'Why did you steal those electronic spares from the Naval Base?'

The Master closed his book slowly. 'At my trial, I made a clean breast of everything. I admitted to all the crimes I had ever committed—at least on this planet.'

'I'm not talking about what you did *before* you were caught,' snapped the Doctor. 'I'm talking about what you were doing an hour ago.'

'An hour ago?' queried the Master switching on a convincing expression of genuine astonishment. 'I'm a prisoner, locked in day and night, for the rest of my life.'

The Doctor got angry. 'Stop play-acting! You've got that fool Trenchard under some sort of influence. What's your game?'

Now the Master smiled. 'My game, Doctor, is to solve the mystery of these vanishing ships. Do you realise how many good and honest sailors have been drowned off this coast in the last two months?'

'I've got that matter in hand, thank you,' said the Doctor. 'I now know the cause, and I hope to find a solution.'

'Except,' said the Master, putting his hand under his book, 'that you are not now going to be available.' From beneath the volume he pulled out the prison officer's gun. 'Goodbye, Doctor.' He levelled the gun at the Doctor's head.

The Doctor allowed himself to fall to one side. As he fell he grabbed the leg of a little coffee table, and hurled it overarm at the Master. It hit him across the side of the face, sending him reeling backwards, the gun dropping from his hand. The Doctor jumped to his feet, looked down at the Master writhing in seeming agony, clutching the side of his head.

'You've probably broken my cheek-bone,' accused the Master.

'You were only going to *kill* me.'

The Master stopped writhing, and seemed to be sliding into a faint. The Doctor moved in closer, to see what he could do to help. Suddenly, the Master sprang into life, picked up the gun again and aimed it at the Doctor's chest. His finger was pressing back the trigger as Trenchard walked in.

'What the hell's going on?' demanded Trenchard, staring at the extraordinary scene.

The Doctor could see that the Master was in two minds. He had only to pull the trigger and his only real enemy, the Doctor, would be dead. But how would he ever explain cold-blooded murder to his new friend, Trenchard?

The Master lowered the gun. 'This man came in here to kill me,' he told Trenchard. 'He knocked out the officer guarding me and took his gun.'

'Really?' said the Doctor. 'Did I do that?' He looked round the room. 'Where did I put the poor fellow whom I knocked out?'

'Don't trust him,' said the Master. 'He's play-acting. The officer is behind the settee.'

Trenchard looked behind the settee, and saw his officer lying there face down. He called to another guard in the corridor. 'Take this visitor to my office immediately. He is under arrest.'

'Won't you take this gun?' said the Master, offering the gun, butt first, to Trenchard. 'And I think the Medical Officer should X-ray my cheek-bone. The Doctor badly beat me up before trying to murder me.'

'Of course,' said Trenchard, taking the weapon. He turned to the prison officer, who had now come in, indicating the Doctor. 'All right, take him away.'

'You know you're making a fool of yourself,' asserted the Doctor.

'I shall speak to you in my office,' Trenchard replied. 'Take him away.' He waited until the Doctor had been led off. Then he turned on the Master. 'What were you going to do?—kill him? I warn you, I won't stand for that sort of thing!'

'I was defending myself,' said the Master, getting to his feet. 'If you refuse to believe that, if you prefer to think of me as a cheap murderer, then that means everything you are doing is wrong.'

Trenchard tried to work that out, but it was all getting too complicated. He very much wished he was back on the North West Frontier with a kindly commanding officer who told him exactly what to do and what to think at any time of day or night. Here, he had to take so many decisions . . .

    .   .   .   .   .

Jo found the château's main gates locked against her, and Prison Officer Snellgrove demanding that she leave the naval Jeep and go with him into the gatehouse.

'This is ridiculous,' she protested. 'I have a perfect right to leave here whenever I wish !'

'The Governor's orders, Miss,' apologised Snellgrove. 'It's not for me to question what you've been up to, but you've got to come into the gatehouse.'

'I haven't been "up to" anything,' she said. 'If you want me to leave this Jeep, you'll have to lift me out !'

'I see,' said Snellgrove. 'A trouble-maker. All right, I shall call my colleague.'

'You can call out the fire brigade if you want,' retorted Jo. 'I'm sitting here till you open those gates.'

Snellgrove walked halfway towards the gatehouse door and called. 'Mr. Crawley, could you come out here a moment, please? There's a visitor causing us bother.'

Crawley emerged from the gatehouse. 'What visitor?' he asked.

'This young lady in the Jeep,' said Snellgrove, turning back to where Jo had been sitting. The vehicle was empty. He swung back towards Prison Officer Crawley. 'Well don't just stand there ! We've got to find her !'

    .   .   .   .   .

The Doctor was hemmed in by two prison officers as he stood before Trenchard's desk.

'You're in very serious trouble,' said Trenchard. 'I'm going to hold you here until this whole thing is cleared up.'

'Is that what the Master told you to say?' asked the Doctor.

'I shall ignore that remark,' said Trenchard, his fists clenched and knuckles whitening. 'You have attacked a prison officer, and attempted to harm a prisoner in my care and protection. As for that UNIT pass of yours, I believe it is a forgery.'

'Don't be an idiot,' said the Doctor. 'Anyone at UNIT Headquarters will vouch for me. If you'll allow me to telephone—'

Trenchard's hand automatically clamped down on the telephone, even though the dial was securely padlocked. 'Prisoners are not allowed to make telephone calls.'

'I'm an *unconvicted* prisoner,' said the Doctor. 'I have a right to telephone a solicitor.'

'Don't quote the law to me, if you don't mind,' said Trenchard. 'I know what I'm doing.' He turned to the prison officers. 'Take this man away.'

The prison officers grabbed the Doctor's arms to wheel him out. The Doctor wouldn't budge. 'You're throwing away your whole career,' he said to Trenchard. 'You'll be a laughing stock.'

'Insulting me won't help you,' said Trenchard. 'You will be properly and humanely treated if you behave yourself, keep your cell clean, and remember to call all prison officers "sir". To that extent this establishment is run as a normal prison. But there is one very considerable difference between this place and other prisons. If you attempt to escape, the prison officers will shoot to kill. I hope that is clearly understood. Now take him away!'

The two prison officers yanked at the Doctor's arms and led him out of the office. He didn't try to protest any more. Clearly Trenchard was so deeply involved that he would never now listen to reason.

As the door closed, the internal telephone buzzed.

Trenchard lifted the receiver. 'Governor here.' A voice at the other end told him that the young lady visitor had left her naval Jeep and was now roaming somewhere in the grounds. Trenchard's voice touched an almost hysterical note as he said, 'Then find her . . . immediately . . . NOW!' He slammed down the 'phone. He was finding it difficult to breathe, and put his hand just under his heart to feel how fast it was palpitating. He knew that he should really visit a doctor, but he was afraid of what he might be told about that heart of his.

With a sudden feeling of total exhaustion, he slumped forward on his desk and buried his face in his hands.

7

Captain Hart Becomes Suspicious

'What exactly will I be looking for, sir?' asked young Lieutenant Ridgway.

'That's a good question,' said Captain Hart. 'But if I knew the answer to that, I wouldn't be sending you there to look.'

At Captain Hart's request, a submarine had arrived from Portsmouth. The captain was Lieutenant Robin Ridgway, R.N., whose boyish looks unnerved Captain Hart; it was incredible to think that a young man who but a few years ago was in his school XI was now entrusted with millions of pounds' worth of naval equipment. He had explained the situation to Ridgway—the sinking of the ships and the continual mechanical problems on the oil-rig. What he had not explained was the existence of the Sea-Devils, because he did not want the young lieutenant to think he was a fool.

Lieutenant Ridgway referred again to the sea-bed charts on the wall of Captain Hart's office. 'I suppose there could be some geological explanation,' he said, more thinking aloud than making a definite statement. 'A movement in the sea-bed, perhaps, or some magnetic phenomenon.'

'I take it you're equipped with hearing and seeing aids?' said Captain Hart.

'Television eyes,' affirmed the lieutenant, 'and underwater "ears". Plus sonar, of course.'

'Good.' Captain Hart stood up, to indicate that the briefing was over. 'I want you to radio me a full report the moment you re-surface.'

'Yes, sir,' said Ridgway.

'All right,' said Captain Hart. 'Carry on. And good luck.'

'Thank you, sir.' Ridgway turned smartly and left the office, with a nod of farewell to W.R.N. Jane Blythe.

Jane waited until Ridgway had closed the door behind him. 'You didn't think it better to tell Lieutenant Ridgway about the Sea-Devils, sir?'

'I don't think they can do any harm to a submarine—*if* they exist,' replied Captain Hart. 'Do you feel I've sent him into danger unforewarned?'

'It's not for me to say that, sir,' said Jane.

'I may be wrong,' said the Captain, 'but look at it this way: if I'd told him what we have only *heard*, and have never seen for ourselves, is it possible he might *imagine* he was seeing Sea-Devils? You see, this way we shall get an objective report.'

'Yes, sir,' said Jane, clearly not convinced that what Captain Hart had done was right. 'If I may mention something else, sir: isn't it time that the Doctor and Miss Grant were back here? They've been gone rather a long while.'

Captain Hart gave thought to that. 'Give Trenchard a ring. Find out whether they got to him, and when they left.'

While Captain Hart took up his favourite position at the window, and watched young Lieutenant Ridgway return to the submarine now berthed alongside the quay, Jane Blythe telephoned Mr. Trenchard. Then she reported to Captain Hart.

'Mr. Trenchard says that they've been to see him, and now gone back to London, sir.' She added significantly, 'He mentioned that he personally called a taxi for them, to take them back to the quay in the village.'

Captain Hart turned slowly from the window. 'He called a taxi for them? What about the Jeep I lent them?'

'Exactly, sir,' said Jane, not wishing to say outright that Captain Hart's friend must be a liar.

He scowled. 'What a peculiar way to carry on. You'd better send someone to collect that Jeep.'

'But sir, why would they take a taxi when they had a Jeep? And isn't it odd that they haven't called back here?'

Captain Hart thought for a moment. Then he went to the clothes-stand and took down his cap. 'You have a very suspicious mind,' he said, allowing himself a little smile. 'I'm going to drop by and see old George. If the submarine reports back, you can reach me at the château.'

. . . . .

While Captain Hart, in thoughtful mood, was driving his car to the château, the Doctor was being brought in handcuffs into the Master's room at the prison.

'Ah, Doctor,' said the Master, producing a hardback chair, 'do sit down.'

Two prison officers pushed the Doctor down in to the chair.

'Do you run this place now?' asked the Doctor.

The Master smiled. 'You might say that I am a privileged guest.' He nodded to the prison officers. In response they unlocked the Doctor's handcuffs.

The Doctor rubbed his wrists. 'Thank you very much.'

But the prison officers quickly grabbed the Doctor's arms, twisted them behind the back of the chair, and replaced the handcuffs so that he was now firmly attached to the chair.

'That'll be all,' said the Master, and the two prison officers departed, closing and locking the door.

'You realise,' said the Doctor, 'that I 'phoned through to UNIT and gave them a full report when Miss Grant spotted you at the Naval Base?'

'I realise,' said the Master, 'that you are lying. If you'd done that, why come back here to investigate in person? Now let's get straight down to business. I've had you brought in here because you may be able to help me.'

'To escape?' asked the Doctor.

'My dear fellow,' the Master laughed, 'I can leave here any time I wish. I only stay on because it makes a useful base for my operations.' He paused for effect. 'I am planning to contact underwater friends.'

The Doctor was genuinely surprised. 'How do you know about them?'

'From the Time Lords' files,' replied the Master, truthfully. 'It's been particularly useful to me,' he went on, 'the way our old friends the Time Lords keep a record of everything.'

The Doctor asked, 'What do you hope to gain by helping the Sea-Devils?'

'Power,' said the Master. 'I shall use them just as I've used the Ogrons.' He smiled reflectively. 'And there will be an additional reward—the pleasure of seeing these humans, of whom you're so fond, being exterminated or made into slaves!'

'What do you want me to do?' asked the Doctor.

The Master turned to the table on which stood a compact black box with dials and controls. 'That, Doctor, is a calling device. It is on the same wavelength as the Sea-Devils' mental waves. I have spent some time here designing it. You might assist me to perfect it. I can manage alone, but with your technical ability it might be easier to complete the task.'

The door opened and a prison officer came in. 'The Governor wants to see you,' he told the Master. 'Come along.'

'I'm having a very important discussion,' said the Master, put out by this interruption.

'Never mind about that,' said the prison officer. 'I said "come on", so jump to it.'

The Doctor was amused. 'Better trot along, old chap,' he advised the Master. 'You're still a prisoner, you know.'

Annoyed, the Master picked up the black box, thrust it under his arm, and went with the prison officer. The door was closed and locked. Alone, the Doctor started to try and slip his hands through the handcuffs. He quickly realised that there was no escape that way.

. . . . .

George Trenchard looked terrified, like a little boy who knows he is about to be caught for doing something terribly wrong. 'I tell you,' he said to the Master, 'Captain Hart's car is at the gates now. He wants to see me.'

The Master was quite calm. He sat in the most comfortable big leather chair in Trenchard's office, the compact black box on his knee. 'Perhaps he wants to talk about your golf tournament.'

'What if he's twigged that something's up?' Trenchard knew that his whole body was twitching with anxiety.

'He's only going to do that if you don't behave normally,' said the Master. 'Pick up that internal 'phone, and tell the gatehouse officers to admit Captain Hart immediately.'

Trenchard hesitated. He felt that he wanted to be sick. 'There's something I didn't mention to you. That girl— she somehow got away. She must be roaming in the grounds somewhere. Naturally, I've got prison officers searching for her.'

'You idiot!' thundered the Master. 'It was the simplest matter to put her under arrest.'

The Master's momentary outburst hurt Trenchard. He had always been used to people being very polite to him. 'There's no need to be rude,' he complained, clearly

84

upset. 'We can't all be geniuses. In any case, it wasn't my fault.'

'I'm sorry,' said the Master untruthfully, realising he had gone too far. 'Perhaps we are both rather on edge. May I suggest that you lift that telephone, and give Captain Hart clearance to enter the grounds? Then, if he asks any difficult questions, you will have to bluff it out, which I'm sure you will do admirably.'

'He may want to see you,' said Trenchard. 'You'd better be reading, or doing exercises or something, in your room. Then I can show you to him on the monitor.'

The Master got to his feet. 'You're forgetting, the Doctor's in there. But I have a much better idea, something that will really put Captain Hart's mind at rest.' He outlined his idea to Trenchard, then had himself led away by a prison officer.

Hand trembling, Trenchard lifted the internal 'phone and told the gatehouse officers not to keep the Captain waiting a moment longer.

Four minutes later Captain Hart was shown in to Trenchard's office. By now, Trenchard had composed himself and greeted his visitor warmly.

'John, my dear fellow,' said Trenchard, 'made up your mind about the tournament?'

'I'm here about the Doctor and Miss Grant,' said Captain Hart. 'You told my secretary that they went by taxi back to the quayside, presumably *en route* for London.'

'That's right,' said Trenchard.

'I lent them a Jeep,' said the Captain, 'and it's now parked down by your gatehouse. I find that a little odd.'

Trenchard felt his mouth suddenly go dry. He had completely overlooked the possibility that the Doctor and Jo had arrived in a vehicle. 'I simply can't explain that,' he said, with all honesty. 'How very strange.'

'There's more,' said Captain Hart, and recounted how Jo Grant had claimed that she saw Trenchard's prisoner freely moving around the Naval Base.

'Absolutely ridiculous,' said Trenchard. 'Young women can be very fanciful, so I'm told.'

Captain Hart now came to the real purpose of his visit. 'Would it be possible for me to see your prisoner, George?'

'All right, old chap,' said Trenchard. He opened the huge oak cupboard doors to reveal the monitor screen and controls. 'Not without a few modern security devices here, you know!' He turned on the monitor screen.

The picture on the screen showed the Master sitting hunched up on a rough wooden chair, reading. There were heavy manacles on both his ankles, connected by a strong chain. He was in a tiny cell that had no window. Captain Hart had seen men in cells before, but nothing quite as primitive and restrictive as this.

'Thank you,' he said, and Trenchard turned off the monitor screen. 'Are the chains absolutely necessary?'

'The man is a vicious criminal,' said Trenchard. 'We feed him properly, of course, and take the chains off for an hour once a week to let him exercise his legs. But I don't run this place as a holiday camp for his benefit.'

'So I see,' said Captain Hart. 'Well, Miss Grant must have been mistaken. I'd better let you get on with your work.'

Trenchard, now in a cheerful mood, showed Captain Hart to the front door. 'I must say, old chap, it was pretty odd of them to leave your Jeep here and take a taxi, but I can't say that I'm really surprised. They seemed a strange couple.'

Captain Hart nodded, and said he'd send someone along to collect the Jeep. Then he got into his car and drove away.

Trenchard hurried back into his office and issued orders for the Master to be brought back to him. He could have had the Master returned to his own room, and then gone to see him there. But it gave Trenchard confidence to talk to people in his own office. Recent events had undermined his self-confidence quite enough, and he intended to build it up again. When the Master entered he was still carrying the black box.

'I convinced him,' said Trenchard, jubilantly. He had no intention of mentioning the Jeep to the Master, in case the Master was angry with him for not hiding it somewhere.

'Congratulations,' said the Master. 'I hope that I played my part satisfactorily?'

'What? Oh, yes, first-class performance, except that you didn't have to *do* anything but sit still reading.' Trenchard went on. 'I had to do all the talking.'

'Which I'm sure you did very well,' said the Master. 'Now I'd better get back to completing this device.' He tapped the black box with his long slender fingers.

'How long before you can have that thing working?' asked Trenchard.

The Master shrugged. 'A matter of hours. Only a few more problems to solve.'

'And you're sure it'll do the trick?'

'This,' said the Master proudly, 'will emit a signal exactly on the enemy's wavelength. It will lure them into a trap, which *you* will set. Think of it, Trenchard, the agents who are sinking these ships will be caught! A grateful country will give you anything you ask for.'

Trenchard blushed. 'I don't want any reward, old man. Just doing my duty. Tell me, have you finished with the Doctor?'

'Not yet,' said the Master. 'He's going to help me complete my work.'

'Good,' said Trenchard, feeling that everything was beginning to turn out all right now. 'Well, I'd better get one of my prison office chappies to escort you back to your room—just for appearances!' He lifted the internal 'phone to call for an officer.

The guard came to take the Master away—and to a surprise that was lying in store for him.

.   .   .   .   .

Jo was not far away when Prison Officer Snellgrove turned and saw the naval jeep empty. She had calculated that the nearest place to hide—the bushes and foliage running along the main outside wall—was too far for her to sprint in the time that Snellgrove was facing Prison Officer Crawley. So she had got out of the Jeep, crawled beneath it and lain flat. From there she heard the two prison officers shouting angrily at each other. She could see Crawley's feet as he hurried back inside the gatehouse to raise the alarm, and Snellgrove's feet as he wandered about aimlessly in circles presumably looking for her in all directions. Then she saw the wheels of the Minimoke come from the direction of the gatehouse.

Crawley's voice called, 'Come on, we'll drive around and find her.'

Snellgrove's voice, close to the Jeep, called back, 'What about this thing?' He must have meant the Jeep, which was standing across the main driveway.

'Leave it,' called Crawley.

Snellgrove's feet ran towards the Minimoke. He got in, and the two prison officers drove away. Jo waited a full minute, then crawled out from under the Jeep and raced towards the foliage. Her first thought was to get back to the Naval Base, and she ran along the inside of the electrified fence that ran parallel with the wall. It soon became clear there was no escape this way. She stopped to catch her breath. If there was no way *out* of the grounds, was there some way *into* the château? Once in there she might find a telephone without a lock on it, or she might be able to break a lock. By a series of quick sprints from one tree or bush to another, she covered the distance from the perimeter to the walls of the château. Suddenly she heard voices of approaching men. She found a little outhouse to hide in and from her hiding place she saw Crawley and Snellgrove and six other prison officers, all carrying shotguns.

'She'll try for the wall,' Crawley was shouting.

One of the other officers asked, 'What if she runs for it?'

Crawley patted his shotgun. 'The governor says she's got to be stopped.'

The men went on their way, towards the outer walls.

88

Jo waited, then emerged from the outhouse. She started to walk round the walls of the château itself. Soon she came to a window with bars across it. This, surely, was the Master's room. Curious, she looked in. Instead of seeing the Master, she saw the Doctor, alone, manacled to a chair, unsuccessfully struggling to free his hands. As soon as she had recovered from her surprise Jo decided that it wasn't fair to raise the Doctor's hopes at this stage, so she crept further along the wall of the huge building. Then she found a little door, no doubt left open by the prison officers who had come out to hunt for her. She quickly ran back to the barred window and tapped on it. The Doctor turned and smiled and at the same time shrugged to show that he was helpless.

Jo had already decided on her plan. First, she pointed to the closed door, put on an angry face and pretended to shout without making a sound. Then she pointed to the Doctor, and then pointed to her own mouth. The Doctor seemed puzzled by this, then got the idea and nodded his head. Finally, Jo pointed to her own wrist watch and held up five fingers—five minutes.

.   .   .   .   .

From the moment Jo vanished from the window, the Doctor started to count the seconds. Each time he got to sixty, he held out straight one of his fingers. When all four fingers and the thumb of one hand were fully extended, he started to shout very loudly.

'Is anyone out there? Can you hear me? I said is there anyone out there?'

The door opened and a prison officer looked in. 'What's all the noise about?'

'The way I'm being kept here is disgraceful,' protested the Doctor. 'You could at least feed me. I'm starving.'

'You'll be fed when the time comes,' said the prison officer, 'so belt up!'

'Please do something about these handcuffs,' said the Doctor, 'they're cutting my wrists.'

The prison officer came across to the chair and looked at the Doctor's wrists. It was at this moment that Jo slipped in from the corridor and hid behind the door.

'There's nothing wrong with them,' said the prison officer.

'You're not wearing them!' retorted the Doctor.

'If you don't stop giving trouble,' said the prison officer, 'you'll be wearing leg irons as well.' He went out, slammed the door and locked it.

'Over there,' the Doctor whispered to Jo, indicating the direction by nodding his head, 'the Master's tool-box.'

On the floor by the table was a box of tools that the Master had been using to construct his black box calling device. Jo found a little file, and after ten minutes of hard work she had filed through one of the links of the handcuffs. The Doctor stood up.

'How do we get out of here?' she asked.

'First,' said the Doctor, going to the tool-box, 'I want to pick these locks,'—this because the cuffs were still heavy on his wrists. He selected a nail, bent it with a pair of pliers, and used the bent nail to pick the mechanism of the bracelets. 'Get behind the door again,' he whispered, then sat back on the chair and put his hands behind it. 'Help!' he shouted, 'I'm in agony.' He groaned convincingly. 'Will somebody please help me!'

The door was flung open. 'What's wrong now?' said the prison officer aggressively.

'The same as before,' said the Doctor, his face contorted in pain. 'These handcuffs are *so* tight . . . it's stopping my circulation . . . I'll get gangrene, lose both my hands . . .' The Doctor slumped forward as though in a faint.

The prison officer crossed to the chair, got out his keys, and bent down to loosen the handcuffs. Suddenly, the Doctor's hand whipped out from behind the chair and delivered a Venusian karate chop. He gently lowered the unconscious prison officer to the floor, then hurried from the room with Jo.

.   .   .   .   .

Ten minutes later the Master was brought back to his room by a prison officer. He had been contemplating all sorts of interesting ways to kill the Doctor, mainly slowly, after the Doctor had finished being of use to him. Instead, he found himself looking at an open door and an unconscious prison officer on the floor.

'Get Trenchard down here immediately,' he curtly ordered the prison officer who had brought him back to his room.

Trenchard arrived in thirty seconds and went pale when he realised what had happened.

'Pull yourself together,' said the Master. 'They've got to be caught quickly! You must arm all your officers and give them orders to shoot to kill!'

'I can't give such an order,' said Trenchard. 'How could I explain it to my men?'

'The Doctor and Miss Grant are enemy agents,' said the Master. 'Criminals!'

'We don't know that that is true,' said Trenchard. 'They have been interfering and a darned nuisance. But they aren't necessarily criminal.'

'If they get their story to the outside world,' said the Master, 'our plans will be ruined—and so will your career!'

'That's still no reason to shoot to kill,' said Trenchard obstinately.

The Master found Trenchard just too exasperating. 'Then shoot to maim, shoot to cripple!'

'One of them,' said Trenchard solemnly, 'is a girl. One does not shoot ladies.'

'Try to understand this, Mr. Trenchard,' said the Master, holding down his desire to hit him for being a sentimental fool. 'If they get away, our work will be stopped. So the enemies of Great Britain, of your Queen, will be able to continue their work of destruction. That means the Doctor and Miss Grant will have helped the enemies of your country. Logically, therefore, they are on the side of the enemy. Do you understand?'

Trenchard did not understand. It was all too complicated. But one thing he grasped: if the Doctor and Miss Grant got back to the Naval Base, or to UNIT, George Trenchard might be punished and disgraced.

'I shall tell my men,' said Trenchard, 'to shoot to kill, but only if it is necessary.'

'Excellent,' said the Master. 'Now issue the order, there's a good man. And for goodness' sake, let's get moving!'

.   .   .   .

On leaving the château by the little open door, the Doctor and Jo raced towards the shore.

Jo asked, 'What do we do when we get to the sea?'

The Doctor kept running. 'There can't be electrified fences there. Perhaps we can make our way along the beach.'

As they approached the sea the ground was more open, and rose up before them. Already they could smell the sea and hear the waves on a beach that they couldn't yet see. There was a shout from somewhere behind them, and Jo looked over her shoulder. The Minimoke, carrying four prison officers, was pursuing them. One of the officers had a loud-hailer and called out to them.

'Stop or we fire! We have orders to shoot to kill!'

'All the more reason,' said the Doctor, running harder, 'to keep going.'

They scrambled up to the top of the rising ground, then found themselves at a cliff edge. Below was a small horse-shoe cove of sand and rocks. From behind, a warning shot was fired.

'Quickly,' said the Doctor, 'over the edge!'

Another loud-hailer boomed at them from behind. 'This is the governor,' called Trenchard. 'I order you to surrender now and you will not be harmed.'

Again Jo looked back. There was another Minimoke, containing Trenchard, the Master and two more armed prison officers. She turned back to face the sea, and started to scramble down the cliff after the Doctor. In a few seconds they were at the foot of the cliff.

'Which way?' she asked.

This part of the beach was flat and sandy. The flat terrain continued to their right, but was closed off with barbed wire. A big notice read: WAR DEPARTMENT. DANGER. MINEFIELD. KEEP OUT. To their left the beach became rocky, but at least had no warning signs

'This way,' said the Doctor, propelling Jo towards the rocks. As they approached they saw the heads of some prison guards bobbing about amongst them. They had descended the cliff further along on the left side, and were now taking up firing positions among the rocks. The Doctor and Jo stopped.

'It's no good, Doctor.' The voice of the Master boomed almost casually at them from a loud-hailer high above on top of the cliff. 'You'll have to give yourself up. You are now hemmed in on all sides. Look out to sea.'

On top of the cliff, Trenchard turned to the Master. 'What do you mean? Look out to sea?'

The Master patted the little black box that he still carried with him. 'I managed to finish this sooner than I expected,' he said. 'So some little time ago I transmitted a signal that will bring to us the people who are sinking the ships.'

Trenchard was confused. 'Whatever are you talking about?'

'Look,' said the Master. He pointed to the waves coming in on the sandy beach.

At first Trenchard thought he was seeing things. Was it some kind of seaweed just under the surface, or fish? Then the heads of six Sea-Devils emerged from the water —huge lizards that walked upright like men as they came in from the sea. Each was armed with some strange gadget that resembled a gun.

Down on the beach the firing from the prison officers stopped. Jo saw that they had seen the monsters, and were themselves running—in panic. One, however, held his position, making it impossible for Jo and the Doctor to escape that way.

'We've got to go through the minefield,' called the Doctor.

The Doctor raced towards the barbed wire, Jo following. There were breaks in the strands, and they were soon through to the other side of the notice that warned them to keep away.

'Doctor,' called Jo, 'we'll get blown to pieces!'

The Doctor had already stopped and produced his sonic screwdriver. 'Possibly not, Jo,' he said, scanning the sand ahead of them with the screwdriver.

As a beam from the screwdriver hit an underground mine, the mine exploded. Jo was knocked off her feet, but otherwise unhurt. By the time she'd got up, the Doctor had advanced to a point beyond the crater caused by the explosion and was already scanning the sand ahead with his screwdriver. Another huge explosion, but Jo was prepared for it this time. She looked back and saw that one of the Sea-Devils was slowly making its way towards the barbed wire.

On the cliff top the Master was watching the Sea-Devil advance toward the Doctor and Jo. 'Kill them, you idiot,' he shouted. 'Fire your gun and kill them!'

'Those terrible creatures,' said Trenchard, 'what are they?'

'Enemy agents,' said the Master, laughing. He called out once more to the Sea-Devil down below. 'Exterminate them, you ugly-looking idiot.' Fortunately, the Sea-Devil could not hear from this distance.

In the minefield the Doctor had by now exploded three mines, and the Sea-Devil was closing in. 'We've got to take a terrible risk,' he told Jo. 'We've got to run a long way forward and hope that we don't set off a mine with our feet, then set one off between us and that thing.' He grabbed Jo's hand and they ran forward together.

With every step Jo wondered if her life was about to end in one terrible explosion. She closed her eyes and gritted her teeth, and followed where the Doctor was pulling her. Then the Doctor stopped. They were now some distance from the approaching Sea-Devil.

'Let's just hope,' said the Doctor, 'that somewhere under the sand there's a mine between us and it.'

He scanned the sand behind them with his sonic screwdriver. Suddenly, there was an enormous detonation, but a few yards in front of the Sea-Devil. It staggered, then retreated back a couple of paces.

'If we're lucky,' said the Doctor, 'it'll think we threw some kind of bomb at it.'

The Sea-Devil had stopped and seemed now to be thinking. Then it turned and started to go back slowly towards the others, who were standing in a group on the beach.

Jo wanted to kiss the Doctor but restrained herself. 'We've got away!'

'We aren't out of this minefield, yet,' said the Doctor.

He started to scan the route ahead, seeking a means of escape from the cove.

8
The Submarine

Lieutenant Ridgway wished that Captain Hart had given him a little more information about what he was supposed to be seeking on the sea-bed. He discussed it with his Second-in-Command, Sub-Lieutenant Tony Mitchell.

'Maybe he doesn't know himself,' said Mitchell.

'I had the feeling,' Ridgway concluded, 'that Captain Hart was holding something back. Still, let's do our best.'

The submarine had been submerged for over forty minutes now, and was nearing the base of the oil-rig. Two sonar ratings were listening attentively to their huge earphones, expecting an echo at any moment from the legs of the giant construction. Sonar, a form of underwater radar, sends out regular signals, and these can be heard as 'pings' over the operator's earphones. If the beam of electronic signals hits anything metal, the signals echo back and the operator hears a 'ping-ping'. The time span between the first and the second 'ping' gives the operator an idea of the distance to the metal object. By prodding with the beam in slightly different directions, the operator may be able to sketch out the outline of a sunken ship or the hull of another submarine.

Ridgway left his periscope and went over to the sonar men. 'Anything yet?'

'No, sir,' one of them said.

But the other operator raised a hand. 'I think I've got something, sir.'

Everyone was quiet. Even through the man's earphones they could all hear a faintly echoing 'ping'. Ridgway turned to the crew in charge of the submarine's special television eye and searchlights. He had held back the order to switch on the searchlights because of the enormous amount of electricity they consumed from the submarine's batteries.

'Television eye on,' he snapped, 'and searchlights.'

The ratings threw the switches. A monitor screen next to the periscope came to life.

'It's getting faster,' said the sonar operator. His companion was now also picking up the echo.

Sub-Lieutenant Mitchell asked, 'Is it one of the legs of the oil-rig?'

'Don't think so, sir,' said the sonar operator. 'I was scanning in the other direction. It's getting really close now!'

There was a sudden shriek of high-pitched 'pings' from the earphones of both sonar operators. They took off their earphones and held them a little way away from their ears. 'I think something's gone wrong, sir,' one of them told Ridgway.

Ridgway rapped out an order: 'Send for sonar maintenance.' A rating hurried off down the single main corridor of the submarine. All at once the earphones went silent.

Then the engines stopped.

For a moment there was complete, eerie silence. Without the throb of engines in the background, there is no sound at all in a submarine. No wind, no waves—utter silence.

'What the—' Ridgway went to an internal 'phone, pressed the button marked 'Engine Room' and said: *'Captain here. What's happening?'*

The voice of the Chief in charge of the engine-room sounded bewildered and confused. *'I've no idea, sir. We're making a complete check. Everything stopped.'*

Sub-Lieutenant Mitchell beckoned to Ridgway. He pointed to the dial that measured their depth under the surface. 'We're going down, fast.'

'That's impossible,' said an astonished Ridgway. He looked at the dial: it was not only possible—it was indeed happening! He turned back to the 'phone. *'Chief, get those engines working right away!'*

'Aye, aye, sir,' said the Chief over the 'phone, with no hint of conviction that he could do it. *'We'll do our best.'*

Mitchell was still staring at the depth dial. 'We're dropping like a stone. Look!' He pointed to the monitor screen.

'Look at what?' asked Ridgway. All he could see on the screen was murky water.

Mitchell was wide-eyed. 'It's gone now. Some sort of giant tadpole. It had legs and arms and it swam.'

One or two of the lower-deck ratings looked uneasily at Sub-Lieutenant Mitchell. In an emergency a Naval officer is not supposed to start seeing imaginary 'giant tadpoles'. He is expected to issue orders and *do* things.

Then the vista of water on the monitor screen went black because the searchlights had cut out. Ridgway swung round to the petty officer in charge of the electricity circuits. 'Get those lights working again!'

The petty officer hurried away to check the fuses.

'We've steadied,' said Mitchell, still watching the depth dial. 'We aren't going down any more.'

'I should think not,' said Ridgway. He took it as a personal affront that so many things had gone wrong at the same time. He 'phoned back to the engine-room. *'How's it going, Chief?'*

'We can't trace the trouble,' said the engine-room Chief, *'but we're checking everything, sir.'*

Ridgway put back the 'phone. 'Now where's the sonar maintainance kilick—'

He stopped in mid-sentence because of the tapping sound from outside. The sound echoed through the submarine, causing every man to turn and look up for'ard.

'We're grating against a wreck,' said Mitchell. Every submariner was aware that there were three wrecks somewhere on the sea-bed at this point.

'Let's hope it doesn't puncture us,' said Ridgway.

The sound was repeated. This time there was nothing irregular or vague about the tapping. Instead, there was a regular metallic thudding.

'Divers?' said Mitchell. 'That's impossible at this depth.'

Ridgway only listened for another moment. Then he gave the order: 'Close all for'ard bulkheads! Sound action-stations!'

Ratings ran down the corridor leading for'ard. The action-stations' klaxon hooters set up their staccato sound throughout the length of the submarine.

In the general hubbub, Mitchell asked Ridgway: 'But what do you think it is?'

'I don't know,' said Ridgway. 'Whatever it is, I think it's trying to get into this submarine.' He turned to Petty Officer Summers who was on navigation control. 'I want someone up top. Will you volunteer?'

'Aye, aye, sir,' said Summers.

'I meant a volunteer,' said Ridgway. 'You don't have to do it.'

'I'll do it,' said the petty officer. 'I'll get ready.' He went to the locker where they kept the emergency escape gear.

The ratings who had gone for'ard started to return. 'We've closed up, sir,' one of them told Ridgway. 'But there was something like a blow-lamp starting to cut through from outside!'

'I believe you,' said Ridgway. 'I'm beginning to believe anything.' He turned to Sub-Lieutenant Mitchell. 'Summers is going to need an R/T unit.'

Mitchell had already thought of that and was checking over a special radio-telephone unit capable of functioning after submersion in water. By now Petty Officer Summers had strapped on to his back a small oxygen tank, and had got rid of his heavy boots and cap. Emergency escape from a submerged submarine involves a man climbing into the upper part of the conning tower, closing behind him its lower hatch. When he opens the upper hatch the air inside the top of the conning tower automatically escapes upwards, and the man shoots up to the surface in the bubble.

'As soon as you surface,' Ridgway told Summers, 'use the R/T to send out a May Day.'

'Yes, sir,' said Summers, taking the R/T unit from Sub-Lieutenant Mitchell.

Ridgway continued, 'Wait until you have been picked up by Naval personnel before you say that someone seems to be boarding us.'

'Yes, sir,' said Summers. 'Can I ask why, sir?'

'The Lords of the Admiralty might not want the world to know exactly what's happened,' said Ridgway. 'Now get on your way, and good luck.'

Summers started to climb the ladder towards the lower hatch of the conning tower. He reached up and tried to turn the opening handle. It would not move.

Ridgway called up to him, 'What's the matter?'

'I don't know, sir,' said Summers. 'It's stuck . . . And it's getting warm.' He whipped his hand away from the handle, 'I mean—hot!'

'Come down immediately,' Ridgway called, and turned to Mitchell. 'Small arms.'

Mitchell got out the one key he never expected to use in a real emergency. It unlocked the special cupboard where rifles and revolvers were kept.

Ridgway called, 'Every man get a gun!' He looked up at the hatch. The whole centre of the hatch had now been cut out with heat; it fell and clanged on to the deck.

'Guns at the ready,' he shouted, getting for himself a revolver. 'Hold your fire until I give the order.'

They waited. Something up in the conning tower was moving around. To attack them it would have to come down the ladder, and that would make it an easy target. But then the unexpected happened. A green scaly arm came down through the hole in the hatch, and in the hand was something like a flashlamp.

'The tadpole,' said Mitchell. 'I told you!'

The thing like a flashlamp suddenly blazed red, and the scaly green hand moved it from side to side. Four ratings screamed, dropped their weapons and fell dead.

Ridgway shouted, 'Fire!'

There was an explosion of rifle and revolver fire in the tiny confined space. The flashlamp again flared its brilliant red and three more ratings fell to the deck. Ridgway realised their position was hopeless.

'Cease fire,' he shouted.

The firing stopped. The scaly hand disappeared, the movement could again be heard from inside the conning tower.

'It's probably turning round,' whispered Mitchell, 'so as to come down the ladder. We can pick it off then.' He levelled his gun at the top of the ladder.

In a strained voice Ridgway said, 'Everybody lay down their guns.'

Mitchell stared at Ridgway. 'Are you crazy?'

Lieutenant Ridgway shook his head. 'Whatever that thing is, it's not on its own. We've got to give in.' He raised his voice again to the men. 'I said, put down your guns!'

*The thing like a flashlamp suddenly blazed red . . . four ratings fell
dead.*

One by one the ratings put their guns on to the deck. Then the feet of a Sea-Devil appeared through the hole in the hatch. It clambered slowly down the rungs of the ladder, then turned round to face the humans.

'You will now obey our orders,' it said. 'This vessel is under our command. You will take us to the Master.'

9
Visitors for Governor Trenchard

Trenchard strode along the corridor to the Master's room. The prison officer on duty jumped to attention and unlocked the door. Before entering Trenchard paused to think exactly what his position was. Losing the Doctor and his friend probably meant ruination of everything. Trenchard was angry with the Master, very angry. Telling lies to Captain Hart was bad enough, but what really upset him were the lies that he had had to tell his own men. After the Doctor and Miss Grant finally escaped through the minefield, Trenchard had had to give some reason to his prison officers why he had let the prisoner out of his cell. 'Tell them,' said the Master, 'that I am the Doctor's friend, and you brought me along so that I could call upon him in friendship to give himself up.' It was a complete and ridiculous fabrication, but that is what Trenchard had had to say to cover up his own guilt. Then there were those extraordinary monsters, and surely that was no coincidence. As he walked into the Master's room he told himself the time had come for a reckoning.

The Master was calmly working on his mysterious black box, and barely looked up as Trenchard marched in.

'You should stand up when I enter,' said Trenchard.

The Master looked up for a moment. 'Really? Why?'

'Listen,' said Trenchard, 'I think this has gone far enough! You said it was foreign agents sinking those ships. You said we'd catch them. You lied to me.'

'My dear Trenchard,' said the Master, carefully adjusting a control on the black box, 'if I'd talked about monsters, would you have believed me?' Because Trenchard didn't answer, the Master looked up again. 'Well, would you?'

Trenchard tried to control his temper. 'I sometimes think that you are the Devil. Now tell me the truth!— you had something to do with those disgusting lizards, didn't you!'

'Those creatures you saw belong to a race of intelligent reptiles with a deadly hatred for Mankind,' explained the Master. 'They have established themselves in the sea. Now they plan to emerge and conquer the world.'

'How on earth do you know all this?'

The Master paused in his work and fixed Trenchard with his eyes. 'Because I am the Master. Didn't they tell you that I'm not human?'

Trenchard scoffed, 'Oh, I can believe that!'

'I mean it seriously, my dear Trenchard. I have two hearts, a temperature of only sixty degrees Fahrenheit, and, if you care to observe closely, my breathing rate is four breaths to the minute compared with your twelve to sixteen. Didn't you check the prison doctor's medical report that was sent along here with me?'

'Don't bother about those things,' Trenchard blustered. 'Couldn't really understand it. But we're getting away from the point. If what you say about those creatures is true, I must notify the Government immediately. I'll leave you with your'—he looked at the black box—'your toy.'

Trenchard turned to go. The Master jumped up, and put his hand gently on Trenchard's arm.

'I implore you, Mr. Trenchard, we must keep this to ourselves a little longer. Hasty action would ruin everything.' He turned and pointed to the black box. 'That thing you call a toy can draw these monsters out of the sea in their thousands!'

Trenchard moved back from the Master, positive now that he was in the presence of the Devil. 'That's *exactly* what we don't want to do!'

'You still don't understand,' persisted the Master. 'We must trap these creatures. The whole of this part of England must be cleared of its civilian population. Then I—but we can let the world know it's all being done by *you*—can draw these lizards out of the sea. Once they're out in the open, the Army and Air Force can slaughter them.'

This made sense to Trenchard. 'Where does the Doctor come into it? Why was he so interfering?'

'He is one of my species,' the Master answered, returning now to work on his black box. 'Except that he's a dangerous criminal. Somehow he has wormed his way into the confidence of the authorities. He can be destroyed all in good time.'

As though nothing more need be explained, the Master continued with his work. For some seconds Trenchard watched him, still wondering. 'Just what does that thing do?' he asked.

The Master said airily, 'It emits a signal that these monsters will find attractive.'

Trenchard came closer to look at the box. 'Make it work.'

The Master seemed reluctant. 'If you wish.' He switched over the on/off control. The box emitted a series of regular bleeping sounds for ten seconds, then went silent.

'I suppose you know what you're doing,' said Trenchard, not very impressed with the demonstration. 'Like having a dog whistle—' As he spoke, the box emitted a quite different series of bleeps. 'What was that?'

The Master quickly switched back the on/off control. 'Some random feedback. I really do need to get on with my work, Mr. Trenchard...'

'That was a message,' accused Trenchard. 'You were receiving a message.'

The Master smiled. 'Well, if it was, it wasn't in any code that I've ever heard before.'

'Switch that thing on again,' said Trenchard.

The Master looked at him, and kept up his friendly smile. 'Whatever for?'

'You sent out a signal—'

'That's right,' said the Master, cutting in. 'As you said, it's like having a dog whistle.'

'Please don't interrupt me,' said Trenchard, as politely as he could manage. 'You sent out a signal, and someone, or some*thing*, replied. Why won't you switch it on again?'

'Are you distrusting me, Mr. Trenchard? I thought we were friends, working together to save this country of yours.'

'I shall repeat my request,' said Trenchard. 'Please switch that thing on again.'

'If you insist.' The Master switched over the on/off switch. Again the box emitted a series of regular bleeping sounds for ten seconds then went silent. Immediately, the Master turned it off. 'There you are. Satisfied?'

'I'm very unsatisfied,' replied Trenchard. 'You should have left it on.'

'Have to care for the batteries,' said the Master. 'I don't want to waste them in a series of useless experiments.' He smiled again. 'Now do you think that I might be allowed to get on with my work?'

Trenchard backed to the door. 'Certainly. We shall talk again soon.' He rapped on the door and the prison officer outside opened it. He urgently wanted to get to a telephone, to tell his superiors what he now believed to be the truth, and to offer his resignation.

Back in his office Trenchard unlocked the little padlock on his outside-line telephone and dialled a London number. He was convinced that what he had heard from the Master's so-called calling device was no 'random feedback'. It was a message, a response to the signal that the Master was transmitting. And that could only mean that the Master and these intelligent lizards were allies.

A telephonist at the Ministry answered him and took her time putting him through to the Minister's secretary.

'I need to speak to the Minister,' he said, 'urgently.'

'Who is that?' said the girl's voice.

'George Trenchard,' he said, 'Prison Governor.'

'Does the Minister know you?' queried the voice.

Trenchard winced at the question. 'He doesn't know me personally,' he answered truthfully, 'but indirectly he employs me.' It was extraordinary that the secretary of the Minister had never heard of him.

'I see,' said the girl. 'Which prison?'

He knew that the girl would not recognise the name given to his one-man prison even if he gave it, so he said: 'The prison that contains the Master. Now will you please put me through to the Minister. It's a matter of life and death.'

'Hold on,' said the girl's voice.

While he waited, his mind turned back to what might happen to him once he had confessed his intrigue with the Master...

The girl's voice was speaking again. 'The Minister says he is very sorry, but he's busy. Is there anything wrong with the Master?'

Trenchard almost put the 'phone down without answering. Clearly the Minister's only interest was the Master, because the Master was a big name and had been in all the newspapers.

'The Master is very well,' said Trenchard. 'The matter of life and death happens to concern the nation.'

'Well, the Minister's very busy,' said the girl. 'Could you write to us about it?'

'Yes,' said Trenchard, with a touch of heavy sarcasm, 'I shall write to you about it.'

'If you send it by first-class post,' the girl said, 'we should get it tomorrow morning, and I'll put it on the Minister's desk straight away.'

'Thank you,' said Trenchard. 'Have you ever thought of living in a country controlled by lizards?'

'Have I what?' said the girl, indicating by the tone of her voice that Trenchard was being cheeky.

'It doesn't matter,' said Trenchard. 'Thank you for being so helpful.'

He put down the 'phone, and thoughtfully replaced its little padlock according to prison rules. He considered telephoning Captain John Hart, to tell him everything. But he already felt too much of a fool. It was one thing to confess to a Minister of State, but he could not bring himself to confess to a personal friend.

As though to remind himself of what a fool he had been, he opened the big oak doors that covered the television monitor and switched on. The Master was concentrating on his infernal black box, busily sending and receiving messages. There was now no question in Trenchard's mind that those strange responding sounds were signals being sent to the Master. At least, Trenchard told himself, he could put a stop to that right away. The black box must be impounded and destroyed.

He knew he could not do it himself. If he went down to the Master's room to take the box away, the Master would talk him out of it, or make him feel foolish again. He decided to send his chief prison officer to get the box, and then he would personally destroy it. Thus decided, he lifted his internal 'phone and pressed the button for the chief prison officer's extension. There was no reply. He tried another extension: again no reply. He tried the gatehouse extension, because there was always someone on duty there. Again he could hear the extension ringing, but there was no response. He went back to the television monitor and turned the control knob that would bring into action other television eyes in different parts of the château. To his horror he saw a picture on the screen of Prison Officer Snellgrove lying on his back in a corridor, eyes wide open. He turned the control knob again and cut to the television eye in the prison officers' mess. Three officers were sprawled across the main dining table and another was slouched on the floor against the wall. He turned the knob once more, and brought in the television eye in the Master's room. The door of the room seemed to be on fire. Through the flames and smoke stepped a Sea-Devil. The Master rose to greet it.

Trenchard knew that everything he feared was true. The Master had not only made a complete fool of him, but the Master's 'friends' had murdered all his staff. He felt in his pocket and found the little key to his desk, opened a desk drawer and took out the old Army revolver that he had kept there since his days in the Army. He checked that it was fully loaded.

As a child Trenchard was often told how his great-great grandfather died. It was during the Indian Mutiny and Major Wilfred Trenchard was the last man left alive in a besieged Army barracks. Knowing that there was no escape, and that the mob outside killed anyone who tried to be taken prisoner, the Major loaded his gun, went outside and shot dead four mutineers before he himself was cut to pieces.

This was what Trenchard must now do. It was his last chance to prove that he was not a failure, and that he was a worthy son of his good family name. He had failed many times in his life, but on this occasion he was going to succeed, even though it meant going down fighting. To give himself a little more courage he recalled that the lizards on the beach were not very fast moving. There were six bullets in his revolver, and with luck he might bag six of these creatures before they knew what was happening and turned on him. His final act of bravery and ability would be written up in the newspapers, and if these lizards were going to try to invade England, George Trenchard would be remembered as the first man, the first *soldier*, who had really tried to stop them. A grateful Government might even put up a little plaque on the outside of the château, over the front door, to remind people that Trenchard had lived, and heroically died, there.

With these thoughts of being remembered as a

courageous man of action, Trenchard opened the door to leave his office. To his horror a Sea-Devil was standing directly outside. Trenchard raised his revolver and tried to pull the trigger. Nothing happened. The Sea-Devil raised its raygun: it flared a brilliant red. Trenchard felt a sudden heat rush through his entire body, choking and blinding him. In his last moment of life he realised that he had forgotten to turn the safety catch of his revolver. Then he fell dead.

10

The Diving-Bell

It took the Doctor and Jo several hours to get back from the minefield to the Naval Base. Once through the mines, they still had to keep under cover in case the prison officers came hunting for them. All told, they walked a good ten miles to return to HMS *Foxglove*. Captain Hart listened patiently to their story, but when they had finished he said :

'I'm sorry, but I don't believe a word of it!'

'Captain Hart,' said Jo, nursing one of her sore feet, 'we haven't walked ten miles to tell you a fairy story.'

'Do you seriously expect me to believe in monsters walking upright and coming out of the sea?' said the captain.

'Ask your friend, Mr. Trenchard,' said the Doctor. 'He saw them. At the same time, you might ask him why he tried to hold us prisoner.'

'I think that I've already troubled Mr. Trenchard quite enough,' said the captain. 'Because you claimed that his prisoner was on the loose I went along to the château and saw him with my own eyes. A man, manacled hand and foot, does not have much opportunity to go masquerading as a naval officer, you know.'

'Manacled hand and foot?' said the Doctor. 'The Master lives in considerable comfort, despite his confinement. What sort of room was he in?'

The captain described the cramped little windowless cell, and repeated that the Master appeared to be chained to the wall.

'They did that to fool you!' said Jo. 'You may be an important man in your Navy, but to me you're just stupid!'

'I must apologise for my young companion,' said the Doctor quickly, before Captain Hart exploded in wrath. 'I think her feet are hurting her.'

'If what you tell me is true,' said Captain Hart, 'Mr. Trenchard is in a conspiracy.'

'That,' said the Doctor, 'is the thrust of our argument.'

The 'phone rang and Captain Hart answered it. He seemed most perturbed by what the caller was telling him. He replaced the receiver and turned back to the Doctor. 'I think this may interest you, Doctor. I despatched a submarine to investigate the sea-bed near to the oil-rig—'

'That's about the first sensible thing you've done!' said Jo.

The Doctor signalled for Jo to keep quiet. 'Let the captain finish what he has to say, Jo.'

'It hasn't reported back,' Captain Hart continued. 'But it's just been spotted by radar heading for the château.'

'How can your people tell that it's the submarine?' Jo asked. 'One spot on a radar screen looks very like another.'

'A very bright observation, Miss Grant,' said the captain. 'But you can tell that a blip is a submarine if it suddenly appears on the radar screen. It means that it's just come to the surface.'

'That's clever,' said Jo.

'Thank you,' said Captain Hart. 'You see, we aren't all stupid in the Navy.' Having made his point he turned back to the Doctor. 'As I said, it's heading for the château. How would you like to accompany me there?'

The Doctor got to his feet. 'Does this mean you're starting to believe us, Captain Hart?'

Captain Hart put on his cap. 'Let's see what George Trenchard has to say. Then I'll make up my mind as to whom I believe. Are you ready, Miss Grant?'

Jo put on her shoes again and followed the captain and the Doctor as they left the office.

.   .   .   .   .   .

The Doctor, Jo and Captain Hart waited at the big gates to the grounds of the château. There had been no answer to the bell and the captain had sent his driver back to the Naval Base to get an explosive charge.

'We could get in,' said the Doctor, 'by way of the shore.'

'If the captain doesn't mind going through a mine-field,' Jo added.

Captain Hart was grim-faced and in no mood for jokes. All the lights in the château were blazing, something he had never seen before, and even from this distance he could see that the great front door was standing wide open. It was unbelieveable that no prison officers had come from the gatehouse to answer the bell on the front gate. 'We shall go in this way,' he said. 'Even at the risk of damaging Government property.'

The captain's Jeep came racing back from the Naval Base. As well as the driver, there were now two petty officers, both explosives experts; they had primers and charges with them.

'Those gates,' said the captain. 'Blow them open.'

The two P.O.s fixed charges to the lock on the gates, then attached wires and uncoiled them from big drums. Everyone stood well back, sheltering behind the Jeep, as the charges were blown. The gates swung open.

A minute later they were all inside the château and Captain Hart was contemplating Trenchard's body. The Doctor had immediately rushed to the Master's room, and now returned to report that it was empty. The jeep's driver and the two petty officers reported finding dead prison officers in many parts of the château.

Captain Hart turned to the Doctor. 'If what you say is true, why did George Trenchard help the Master?'

'What would you say was Trenchard's strongest characteristic?' the Doctor replied.

Hart shrugged. 'I don't know. Perhaps patriotism, love of country.'

'Exactly,' agreed the Doctor. 'My guess is that the Master utilised that in some way.' He kneeled down to examine Trenchard's body, to see if he had been killed the same way as the man on the oil-rig.

'Anyway,' said Hart, 'he's gone now. But he's still got his gun in his hand. At least he went down fighting.'

The Doctor looked at the revolver clutched in Trenchard's hand, and noticed that the safety catch was still in position. Unseen by Captain Hart, the Doctor turned the safety catch so that no one would ever know about Trenchard's last fatal mistake. 'Yes,' he said, 'he was a brave man.'

Captain Hart went into Trenchard's office, lifted the 'phone and realised that the dial was padlocked. 'Find some tools,' he called to his driver, 'and get this padlock broken.'

'Allow me,' said the Doctor. He produced his sonic screwdriver and destroyed the little padlock.

'What on earth is that gadget?' asked Hart, as he started to dial.

'It isn't from Earth,' said the Doctor.

Jo asked, 'Why didn't you use it when you wanted to 'phone before?'

The Doctor answered her quietly, 'I hardly think Mr. Trenchard would have approved.'

Captain Hart was talking to the Naval Base. He asked for ambulances to be sent to take away the dead prison officers. Then he listened intently as he was told something by the person he was speaking to. When they had finished he replaced the 'phone and spoke to the Doctor.

'The submarine has been traced, leaving here and making straight for the oil-rig.'

'The Sea-Devils must have taken it over,' said Jo.

'No doubt,' said Captain Hart, clearly sceptical that lizards could be in command of a British submarine. 'It has now disappeared from the radar screen again close to the oil-rig, so that means it's submerged.'

'Then there's only one course open to us,' said the Doctor. 'Can you provide me with a diving-bell?'

'Whatever for?' asked the captain.

'Somebody has got to go down there and try to make contact with these creatures,' said the Doctor.

Jo watched as Naval ratings prepared the diving-bell. It was a huge cylindrical object, the shape of an oil-drum but large enough to carry two or three people. Right now it hung suspended a few feet above the deck of the special diving-bell mother-ship. They were anchored about two miles out at sea, exactly over the last point where the submarine was traced by sonar.

The Doctor and Captain Hart came along the deck. The Doctor smiled when he saw Jo. 'The captain's still trying to convince me that I shouldn't go down.'

'You're not a trained diver,' said the captain.

'But I *am* a scientist,' said the Doctor. 'So what I don't know I should quickly learn.' He called to the petty officer in charge of the preparations. 'Ready for me, yet?'

'Ready we are,' said the petty officer. 'Will you climb in now, sir?'

'Gladly,' said the Doctor. He turned to Jo. 'Don't worry, I'll be back in no time.' He gave a wave to Captain Hart then climbed into the hole at the bottom of the diving-bell. As soon as the Doctor was inside, ratings slammed home a stout metal hatch that covered the hole and pulled tight clamps all round it. The Doctor's face appeared at one of the little observation portholes in the side of the bell, and smiled down at Jo. She waved, not with great enthusiasm.

'Ready on the winch,' called the petty officer.

The diving-bell hung from a deck crane. First this was swung round, so that the bell now hung over the sea. Then the sailor at the winch pulled a lever: a drum of coiled metal rope started to turn, and the diving bell slowly descended into the sea. Jo went to the side rail to watch as the bell touched the water, sank into it, was visible for a few moments through the water, then disappeared altogether.

'You'll get cold here,' said Captain Hart. 'Come into the communications cabin. We can chat to the Doctor by telephone.'

Jo followed the captain along the deck and into a small cabin filled with electronic equipment. The captain sat himself at a desk and switched on a loudspeaker and microphone. '*Hart speaking,*' he said into the microphone. '*Can you hear me all right?*'

'*Extremely well,*' came the Doctor's voice. '*There are some fish here taking considerable interest in me.*'

'*You must make a pleasant change for them,*' said the captain. '*Life down there must get pretty monotonous.*'

The Doctor did not reply.

'*Are you all right?*' asked Captain Hart.

The Doctor's voice replied clearly. '*Fine. But I was looking through the porthole. I thought that I saw something. How deep am I?*'

'*You're on rapid descent,*' said Captain Hart, '*so you're almost at sea-bed now.*'

Again, no reply. Captain Hart smiled to Jo, and Jo smiled back.

'Must give him a chance to look through the porthole,' said Captain Hart after some seconds had passed. 'Like a cup of tea?'

'I don't think so,' said Jo. She waited a few more seconds. 'Hadn't you better check if he's all right, again?'

'Suppose so,' said Hart. He turned back to the microphone. '*What did you think you saw, Doctor?*'

The Doctor's face appeared at one of the little observation portholes, and smiled down at Jo.

No reply.

'Doctor,' said Hart, 'are you still hearing me all right?'

No reply.

Jo went to the microphone. 'Doctor! Will you please answer!'

Silence.

Captain Hart jumped up and hurried out of the cabin, Jo following. By the time she had caught up with him, he had issued the order for the diving-bell to be winched up at fastest possible speed.

It took five minutes, with the winch drum turning at top speed, before the diving-bell came burbling up through the water. The crane arm was swung inboard, and then the winch operator gently brought the diving-bell down to within a few feet of the deck. The petty officer and his ratings tore at the clamps holding the hatch. The moment the hatch fell open, the petty officer poked his head up inside the diving-bell. Then he withdrew his head and turned to Captain Hart.

'It's empty, sir,' he said. 'The Doctor's vanished.'

I I

'Depth Charges Away!'

When the forlorn Captain Hart and Jo returned to the captain's office at the Naval Base, it was to find a portly gentleman seated at the desk having a very hearty breakfast.

'Robert Walker,' he announced himself, holding his hand across the remains of bacon-and-egg to be shaken. 'Parliamentary Private Secretary.'

'How do you do,' said Captain Hart, a little surprised to find his office being used as a restaurant. He introduced Jo, but Walker took no interest in her.

Walker explained that the Government had put him in

complete charge of the situation. He buttered toast and added to it rough-cut marmalade while Captain Hart reported on the loss of the submarine and now the mysterious disappearance of the Doctor.

'There's no question as to what must happen now,' said Walker, his mouth full of toast. He was about to say more, but Jane Blythe hurried in with a pot of fresh coffee and that took all of Walker's immediate interest. 'Thank you,' he said, opening the lid to peer inside. 'It still doesn't look very strong to me.'

'I'll take it back to the steward if you wish, Mr. Walker,' said Jane.

Walker raised his hand in protest. 'This is a time of emergency, a time when we must all make sacrifices. Weak coffee will have to suffice.' He turned back to Captain Hart. 'Where was I?'

'You were just about to butter that bit of toast,' said Jo, pointing to some uneaten toast.

'And you were going to say,' said Captain Hart, 'what must happen now.'

'Ah yes,' and Walker started buttering more toast. 'This is a time for an all-out attack. In your absence I, on behalf of Her Majesty's Government, have ordered a fleet of ships and planes to the centre of the trouble. We shall totally exterminate the monsters that you described in your report to the Minister.'

Captain Hart was shocked. 'The submarine is down there—and the Doctor too, if he's still alive.'

'As I said earlier,' Walker went on, 'we must make sacrifices.' He looked over to Jo. 'Could you pass me the marmalade, my dear?'

. . . . .

The Doctor and the Master stood side by side facing the Chief Sea-Devil. They were in the main hall of the Sea-Devils' vast underwater shelter. The walls, doors, and even what furniture existed were all made of iron. The Chief Sea-Devil sat on an iron throne, flanked by his guards.

'This is our planet,' said the Chief Sea-Devil. 'My people ruled Earth when Man was only an ape.'

'I know what happened,' said the Doctor. 'I have met your people before, in caves in another part of England. You feared that the arrival of another smaller planet, coming towards Earth from Space, would make life on the surface impossible. So you built these shelters. But the smaller planet did not harm Earth; it went into orbit round it, and is now the Moon.'

The Chief Sea-Devil nodded. 'For that reason our temporary hibernation was prolonged by millions of years. 'This oil-rig'—he pointed upwards—'has awoken us. Now we intend to reclaim what is rightfully ours.'

The Master spoke up. 'With my help you can do that! Mankind will be destroyed or enslaved.'

'Is it not better to try for peace?' said the Doctor. 'Why not share the planet with Man?'

The Master laughed. 'Don't listen to this person, I beg you. Man is busily exterminating every other species on the planet. Can you deny that, Doctor?'

The Doctor could not deny the truth. 'Man has been foolish. It is true that many species have been wiped out—'

'The dodo,' cut in the Master, 'the passenger pigeon, the great auk, the blue buck, marsupials in Australia . . . In the first seventy years of this century, humans have totally destroyed more than seventy species!'

'I admit that,' said the Doctor. 'But Man can learn.' He turned back to the Chief Sea-Devil. 'Allow me to return to the surface, to arrange peace between you and Mankind.'

'If you release him,' said the Master, 'he will return with ships that can drop underwater bombs to destroy you. The Doctor is your most deadly enemy. I urge you to kill him now!'

The Chief Sea-Devil raised his green scaly hand. 'We appreciate your friendship,' he told the Master, 'but you speak too much. I must now think.'

The lids of the Chief Sea-Devil's eyes slowly closed,

and for a full minute he seemed almost to be asleep. As he thought he gently rocked forwards and backwards. Then the eyes opened again. He was looking at the Doctor.

'You will negotiate a truce between my people and the humans,' he told the Doctor. 'We shall return you to the shore unharmed.' He signalled to his guards. 'Prepare the capsule.' He referred to the pod-like capsule into which the Doctor had been drawn from the diving-bell.

'I warn you,' shouted the Master, 'you are throwing away the control of this planet. These humans will never make peace with you—'

The Master's words were drowned by the sound of a huge underwater explosion close to the Sea-Devils' shelter. It was followed by another and then another even more violent explosion that rocked the shelter. One of the Sea-Devils went to an electronic screen set in the metal wall, and turned it on. The screen showed twenty or more little blobs of glowing light. He pointed to the screen. 'Ships on the surface above us. The humans are attacking us.'

'You see,' said the Master. 'This is what the humans are really like.'

The Chief Sea-Devil stood up, gripping the arm of his metal throne as more explosions rocked the shelter. He pointed at the Doctor. 'Take him away and kill him!'

Sea-Devil guards immediately gripped the Doctor's arms to drag him away.

'Listen to me,' called the Doctor, but already he was being dragged out of the main hall.

The Chief Sea-Devil issued orders. 'Send our best swimmers to the surface. Destroy each of these ships. Let no human sailor survive!'

The guards were about to carry out the order, but the Master called: 'No! Wait. The humans will retaliate by dropping underwater bombs from their flying machines, and against that you have no defence.'

There were three more violent explosions, dangerously close now.

'Would you have us killed?' asked the Chief Sea-Devil.

'There is a better way,' said the Master. 'To help revive the rest of your people from hibernation, I need time. We can gain that if we make the humans believe they have won. Send to the surface one dead member of your species. That will convince the humans that their underwater bombs have been successful, and they will go away.'

'None of my people have been killed,' said the Chief Sea-Devil.

The Master looked round at the guards, finding it difficult not to smile. 'Then you will have to arrange that, won't you?'

• • • • •

His arms pinioned behind his back, the Doctor was dragged from the main hall by two Sea-Devil guards. As they went down a long metal corridor, no doubt to the Doctor's place of execution, the explosions outside shook the shelter so badly that a metal plate fell from the roof and knocked out one of the Sea-Devils. With one arm free, the Doctor was able to spring loose from the other guard. The surviving guard raised his raygun to fire, but already the Doctor had grabbed the raygun of his fallen comrade. The Doctor fired first. The surviving guard survived no more, and fell dead next to his unconscious companion. The Doctor sprinted down the corridor and quickly found himself in what seemed to be the penal section of the shelter. Lieutenant Ridgway and Sub-Lieutenant Mitchell stared at the Doctor through the bars of a cage. 'Who the blazes are you?' asked Lieutenant Ridgway not without reason.

'We'll leave the introductions till later,' said the Doctor. 'Now stand back.'

He aimed the Sea-Devil's raygun at the lock of the cage, and pressed the control button. The lock disintegrated into liquid metal. Ridgway and Mitchell were free.

'Those explosions,' said Mitchell, 'they've stopped.'

It was true. There hadn't been a detonation for at least two minutes.

'Well let's not stop and chat about it,' said Ridgway. 'We've got to find the sub. I think it was this way . . .'

Ridgway led the trio down a maze of corridors, trying to recall how he and Mitchell were brought to the cage. Because Ridgway was now the pathfinder, the Doctor gave him the Sea-Devil's raygun.

'The sub was drawn by some force into a kind of underwater harbour,' said Ridgway, as he turned down another corridor. He stopped dead. At the end of the passage was a Sea-Devil, its back turned to them. 'What do you think is the range of this raygun?' he asked the Doctor.

'I've no idea,' said the Doctor.

'Well,' said Ridgway, 'it isn't very gentlemanly to shoot a fellow in the back, but here goes.' He aimed the raygun, pressed the control, and the Sea-Devil leapt into the air then fell heavily.

They raced down the corridor, Mitchell collecting the fallen Sea-Devil's raygun as they went. The corridor opened into a vast cavern, the bottom half of which was full of water. Sitting in the water was the submarine. A metal gangplank led from the water's edge to the conning tower. As the Doctor and the two officers ran up the gangplank and started to descend into the conning tower, they heard distantly a hooter blowing at regular intervals.

'Their version of "action-stations",' said Mitchell, as he climbed into the conning tower. 'They probably just realised we're missing.'

At the bottom of the tower, Ridgway paused and looked down through the hole in the hatch. He could just see the lower part of a Sea-Devil standing guard. He aimed the raygun and pressed the control. Even before the Sea-Devil had fallen to the deck, Ridgway had jump-climbed down the ladder into the main control area.

Petty Officer Summers looked at Ridgway, beaming. 'Good to see you back, sir.'

'Any more of these creatures on board?' asked Ridgway.

'No, sir,' said Summers, 'only the one you just killed. The lads are all locked up aft. I'll go and release them.'

In under five minutes the submarine was again fully operational, every man at his post. The big moment of tension was when Ridgway gave the order to start the engines. Would the same mysterious force still restrain them?

But the engines started, and soon Ridgway had the submarine submerged and starting to reverse out from the underwater cave.

Then the Sea-Devils retaliated. When the submarine was halfway backed out from its underwater prison, with the propellers revolving in reverse at full speed, a force field set up by the Sea-Devils started to draw it back into the cavern.

'It's no good, sir,' the engine-room Chief told Lieutenant Ridgway, 'I can't get any more power out of the engines.'

'There's only one thing to do,' said the Doctor. 'Fire one of the forward torpedoes.'

'Are you mad?' said Ridgway. 'When the torpedo strikes the wall of the cave, it'll blow off the front of the sub!'

'Or,' maintained the Doctor, 'push us out of the cave like a cork out of a bottle.'

Ridgway gave it only two seconds' thought. If the Sea-Devils took them prisoner again, he was convinced they would all be killed. This way, there was just a chance. 'Arm torpedo number one,' he ordered.

Seconds later the report came back that torpedo number one was primed and ready.

'Fire,' said Ridgway.

For some seconds nothing happened beyond the slight remor of the sleek cigar-shaped cylinder leaving its tube. The engines were still pulling full speed in reverse.

No one spoke as they waited for the explosion. Then it

happened. The shock waves reverberated through the submarine.

.   .   .   .   .

The Sea-Devils watching the submarine on their underwater radar saw it suddenly leap backwards from the cavern, pushed out by the force of the explosion of the torpedo. Very soon it was out of reach of their magnetic force-field.

'The humans,' said the Chief Sea-Devil, 'will soon be told of our trick. The guard whom we killed and sent to the surface died in vain. They will attack us again.'

'I agree,' said the Master. 'Personally I would have liked more time to prepare. But it does seem that now is the moment for you to attack the Naval Base in force. Once you are established there, you will have taken the first step towards the reconquest of your planet!'

12

Attack in Force

Parliamentary Private Secretary the Right Honourable Robert Walker regarded the Doctor and Lieutenant Ridgway across the lunch of cold chicken, sauté potatoes, mixed salad with French dressing, and chopped celery that was laid before him. All Captain Hart's files and ink bottles and pencils had been removed from the desk top in order to turn it into a dining table for the man from the Government.

'May I congratulate you,' Walker said, bayoneting a slice of chicken on to the prongs of his fork, 'on a remarkable escape. As soon as I've finished my lunch, I shall order that atomic weapons be used against these monsters.' He popped the morsel of chicken into his mouth and started to chew.

The watching Sea-Devils saw the submarine suddenly leap backwards from the cavern.

'With all respect,' said Captain Hart, who stood to one side next to Jo, 'I doubt that the Doctor would agree to that.'

'I disagree very much,' said the Doctor. 'This is a time to make peace, not war. These creatures have underground bases all over the world. You must share the planet with them.'

'We hardly know how,' said Walker, prodding about in his mixed salad to find a slice of tomato, 'to share the planet with each other, my dear fellow. Look at the Middle East, or Northern Ireland. If we could catch some of these things alive and put them in a zoo, to that I could agree. But the rest must be destroyed.'

'These are intelligent creatures,' the Doctor protested. 'Wouldn't you prefer to be known as Walker the Peace-maker, than the man responsible for the deaths of millions of people?'

'Won't be any deaths,' said Walker, sipping his white wine appreciatively, 'except for them.'

'I believe that the Doctor's right,' said Captain Hart. 'I've checked with Brigadier Lethbridge Stewart of UNIT about the creatures that were in those caves in Derbyshire. If they all start to emerge from their underground shelters throughout the world, we won't know what's hit us!'

Walker buttered a bread roll. 'It's really possible, Doctor, to communicate with these creatures?'

'I can vouch for that,' said Lieutenant Ridgway. 'They interrogated Sub-Lieutenant Mitchell and myself. They wanted to know about the weapons we have, and how many millions of people inhabit the world. They're intelligent—too intelligent, if you ask me.'

'As it so happens,' said Walker, 'I haven't asked you. But I have noted what you say.' He popped a piece of buttered bread into his mouth. 'All right, Doctor. Let's see what you can do.' He raised his wine glass to his lips.

'Thank you,' said the Doctor. He swung round to Captain Hart. 'I shall need the diving-bell again.'

'Doctor,' said Jo, 'couldn't someone else go down this

time?' She looked at Walker. 'What about you, sir? It's a job for a trained diplomat.'

Walker almost spilt his wine. 'I'm sorry, my dear, but I get terribly sea-sick. It's just one of those little problems that one has to put up with in life.'

.   .   .   .

The Doctor, Jo, Captain Hart, and the Rt. Hon. Robert Walker left the administrative building and walked towards the waiting diving-bell vessel.

'Not a bad day for a little jaunt out to sea,' said Walker, adding quickly to Jo, 'for those who don't get sea-sick, of course.'

'I'd hardly call this a "little jaunt",' said Captain Hart. 'After those depth charges you had dropped, sir, I imagine the Sea-Devils will be in no mood to receive visitors—'

He stopped short because Jo was pointing wildly towards the quay. 'Look!' she screamed. 'Sea-Devils!'

Sea-Devils came swarming up from the water on to the quay. Those who had already landed and secreted themselves in hiding places now appeared. Two Sea-Devils came running towards the group of humans now caught unprotected in the open area between the administration building and the boat.

Walker shrieked, 'We come in peace! Don't kill us!'

As one Sea-Devil raised its raygun to fire at Walker, the Doctor leapt at it and felled it with a Venusian karate chop. The other Sea-Devil came up behind the Doctor, and brought its hand down on to the Doctor's head. He fell unconscious on to the concrete. The Sea-Devil raised its gun to exterminate Walker, Hart, and Jo.

'Stop!' It was the voice of the Master. He came running from the quayside. 'They may be useful as slaves.' He looked down at the Doctor. 'And so may he.'

.   .   .   .

Jo, Captain Hart, and the Rt. Hon. Robert Walker were locked in a stationery cupboard in the administration building. It had shelves piled with typewriting paper, envelopes, and other office equipment. By peeping through the keyhole they had seen that a Sea-Devil was standing outside on guard. Captain Hart was now standing on a shelf using a twopenny piece as a make-do screwdriver to remove the screws from a ventilator grille.

'If we escape from here,' said Walker, 'we're only going to make them angry.'

'If we don't escape from here,' replied Captain Hart pointedly, 'we are only going to be killed.'

Walker pulled from his jacket pocket a little packet of sweets and helped himself to one. 'Why didn't they lock the Doctor in here with us?'

'Probably,' said Jo, 'because the Master needs his help. Why don't you offer your sweets round?'

Walker blustered, and tried to think of a reason. 'They are specially made to suit my taste. I don't think you'd like them.' He pushed the packet back into his pocket.

Captain Hart carefully lifted away the ventilator grille. 'There's a shaft leads straight outside,' he said, 'but it isn't very big.'

Jo climbed up on to the shelf. 'I'm the smallest,' she said. 'Give me a hand.'

Captain Hart looked at her. 'You realise the danger?'

'You have just told us,' she reminded him. 'If we don't escape we'll be killed. Help me get into that hole.'

As the Captain helped Jo into the ventilator shaft, Walker watched on from below, and secretly helped himself to another sweet.

.   .   .   .   .

Jo dropped down cautiously from the outside opening of the ventilator shaft. She was at the side of the administration building. At the other end of the roadway she could see five or six naval ratings walking along with their hands raised, guarded by two Sea-Devils. The group went out of sight behind an outbuilding.

The problem was, she told herself, where to find the Doctor? The Master had saved the Doctor's life, and that meant he must be using the Doctor for some purpose. Then she remembered where the Master had gone when he was brought into the Naval Base by the late Mr. Trenchard: the electronic stores. She worked her way cautiously along the wall of the building, and was relieved to find a signpost giving directions to various parts of the base. One finger in the signpost pointed towards 'Stores'. She made her way in that direction, keeping a careful look out for Sea-Devils. Hiding whenever she saw one of the monsters, sprinting quickly from the shelter of one hiding place to another, it took her a long time to reach her destination. The door of the stores shed was open, but she thought it wisest first to try and look inside before entering. She found a window, and peeped inside.

The Master and the Doctor were working on some elaborate piece of electronic equipment. Standing watching them was a Sea-Devil; it kept its raygun aimed at the Doctor all the time as he worked. Jo could just hear what the Master was saying.

'. . . With this, we shall be able to re-activate *homo reptilia* all over the world.'

Jo remembered hearing the Doctor use that term to describe the monsters that had been found in the caves in Derbyshire. It also described their underwater cousins.

'How will that benefit you?' said the Doctor.

'Us,' said the Master. 'I can make you a partner . . .'

The Master went on talking about how he and the Doctor would rule Earth through the Sea-Devils. The Doctor, meanwhile, had caught sight of Jo's face at the window, and was secretly signalling to her. While pretending to listen to the Master, the Doctor pointed to the Sea-Devil, then to the electronic equipment, and finally pulled a face of agony. Jo understood, and nodded. Then the Doctor put his hand behind his back, where Jo could see it, and splayed out his four fingers and thumb. She tried to work out what he meant. Then she remembered the way she had signalled to the Doctor when he was manacled to a chair in the Master's room at the château. So, in five minutes from now the Doctor was going to do something that would put the Sea-Devils in agony.

Jo worked her way back to the administration building, dodging Sea-Devils, taking cover whenever she could. Fortunately, no Sea-Devils had been left on guard at the main entrance. But when she got inside, and was making her way to the stationery cupboard, she saw that the Sea-Devil guarding the cupboard door was still on duty. It saw her at the same moment. The Sea-Devil raised its raygun and took aim. Then, suddenly, it recoiled as though hit by high voltage electricity. It crashed to the floor, writhing in agony. Jo kicked the fallen raygun out of the Sea-Devil's reach, and turned the lock in the door of the cupboard.

'Well done, Miss Grant,' said Captain Hart. 'After you, Mr. Walker.'

Walker stayed where he was. He was quivering with fear. 'This is only going to annoy them,' he said. 'Have you no thought for others? We should make peace, not war.'

'But not peace at any price,' said Captain Hart, and shoved Walker ahead of him out of the cupboard. 'Now let's release the ratings—and start winning!'

．　　　　．　　　　．　　　　．

When the Doctor switched on the power connected to the re-activation unit, the Chief Sea-Devil watching the work also fell in agony to the floor. Fortunately for Jo, the Master was in another section of the stores at the time, looking for additional equipment. This allowed the Doctor to keep on the power for a full minute. Then the Master returned and saw what had happened.

'You idiot!' stormed the Master.

'Why, what's wrong?' said the Doctor, turning round and pretending only now to notice that the Chief Sea-Devil was in acute pain on the floor. 'Good grief,' he said, 'do you think he's having a fit?'

The Master yanked the power lead from its wall

socket. Instantly, the Chief Sea-Devil recovered, and started to get to its feet.

'You overloaded the re-activater,' said the Master. 'We want this thing to revive the Sea-Devils who are in deep hibernation, not to knock out those who are already fully awake!'

The Doctor examined his arrangement of the electrical circuits. 'Hm,' he pondered, 'too much in-flow of the neutrons. We'll have to fix that.'

'It *was* fixed,' said the Master. 'Do you realise you must have temporarily knocked out every Sea-Devil in the base?'

'How terribly thoughtless of me,' said the Doctor. He turned and smiled at the Chief Sea-Devil. 'You will, I hope, forgive me?'

'We never forgive,' said the Chief Sea-Devil, levelling his raygun at the Doctor. 'We are the rulers of this planet. It was ours millions of years before you apes developed and took it over from us. We shall destroy all Mankind, and all mammals. Only the reptiles shall survive—'

The Chief Sea-Devil's sentence ended there because a bullet from a .44 service rifle, travelling at three times the speed of sound, and fired by one Petty Officer Myers, had just entered and destroyed its brain. The Chief Sea-Devil fell backwards, dead before its huge body hit the floor.

Petty Officer Myers stood in the doorway and lowered his rifle. 'Is one of you gentlemen the Doctor?'

'I am,' said the Doctor. 'What's happened?'

'All these creepy-crawly things had some sort of a fit,' said the petty officer. 'It lasted long enough for Captain Hart to release all us prisoners, and get our guns back to us. Now that we've fought off the monsters Captain Hart would now like to see you, sir.'

'Yes, of course,' said the Doctor. 'I want you to keep an eye on this man,' and he indicated the Master. 'Under no circumstances may he leave here. Where is the captain?'

'Admin. block,' said the petty officer. He looked at the Master distastefully. 'Don't worry, sir. I'll look after him.'

The Doctor hurried away.

The Master looked down at the Chief Sea-Devil's body. 'You have just killed one of the most intelligent creatures that ever walked on this earth,' he told Petty Officer Myers.

'Really, sir?' said the petty officer. 'They look like big frogs to me.'

The Master turned to the petty officer. 'You've misunderstood the whole situation. Are you aware of that?'

The petty officer found that the Master was staring straight into his eyes. He did not feel very sure of himself. 'I've misunderstood, sir?' he said.

'I am the Master, and you will obey me. Do you understand that?'

Petty Officer Myers felt a strange swimming sensation in his mind. 'You are the Master,' he repeated slowly, 'and I shall obey.'

'Unload your rifle,' said the Master, still fixing the petty officer's eyes with his steady stare.

Like a sleep-walker, the petty officer unloaded his service rifle.

'Put your rifle to one side,' said the Master.

The petty officer obeyed the command.

'I am sorry to leave you,' said the Master. 'But I have urgent business elsewhere. Remain exactly where you are.'

'I shall remain exactly where I am,' said the petty officer.

The Master, however, did not hear the petty officer's words because he was already running as fast as he could towards the quay, taking the re-activating device with him.

.   .   .   .   .

On the way to the administration building, the Doctor had to take cover as fighting broke out between naval ratings and a small pocket of Sea-Devils who were now trying to escape. There were three Sea-Devils hiding behind a naval bus, using rayguns on the sailors. The sailors, numbering twenty, kept up a volley of fire. Very soon another group of sailors, all armed, worked their way in behind the Sea-Devils. The battle was quickly over.

The Doctor continued on his way, then from the corner of his eye saw the Master racing towards the quay. The Master jumped into a motor-boat, started the engine and roared out towards the sea. The Doctor realised there was no time to call for help. He ran to the quay, found another motor-boat, jumped into it, and fired the motor.

The Master drove his boat in a dead straight line towards the oil-rig. Once in the open sea both boats had to contend with choppy waves; the Doctor, being in the wake of the Master's boat, also had to contend with the wash of the boat he was pursuing. Frequently, the Master slewed his boat from side to side, to put up more wash against the oncoming Doctor, and possibly to overturn the latter's boat. As his small craft bucked about like a wild horse, the Doctor steered straight ahead. Because the Master zig-zagged to put up more wash, and because the Doctor kept straight ahead, by the time that they neared the oil-rig the Doctor's boat had caught up with the Master. The Doctor overhauled his boat, then came across his bows. In the moment that the two boats touched, the Doctor leapt into the Master's boat, pushed the Master aside and stopped the motor.

'You're coming back with me,' he told the Master.

'On the contrary,' said the Master. 'I think you are coming with me. They're waiting for us.'

The Master indicated the sea around them. It was swarming with Sea-Devils. Now, coming up from below, were two of the pod-like capsules into which the Sea-Devils had drawn the Doctor from the diving-bell.

'This time,' the Master smiled, 'I don't think they will listen to you at all, Doctor. You will work on the task that I set you. After that, neither I nor my friends will have any further use for you.'

Escape

Captain Hart's office was a mess. In the fighting that took place after Hart had released the sailor prisoners, parties of naval ratings with guns had searched every part of the Naval Base seeking Sea-Devils. A group of Sea-Devils had been found in Captain Hart's office, and a battle had raged in there. The burning effect of the Sea-Devils' rayguns was to be found on the door and walls, and rifle bullets had smashed through the furniture and windows. As ratings lifted out the bodies of dead Sea-Devils, Captain Hart was trying to telephone his superiors in London, but the 'phone wires had been cut in the fighting.

'There is no need to speak to anyone in London,' said Mr. Walker. 'I can tell you what must be done. We need a massive underwater nuclear strike—immediately!'

Captain Hart put down the useless telephone. 'I couldn't do that without orders from the Admiralty.'

'Leave the question of orders to me,' said Walker.

Jo spoke up. 'Shouldn't we wait till the Doctor gets here? You ought to listen to his opinion.'

'According to your very own words,' Walker said to Jo, 'your friend the Doctor was last seen helping the enemy. In a time of war, people get shot for that.'

Jane Blythe hurried in. 'Sir,' she addressed Captain Hart. 'I've found out where the Doctor is. One of the ratings saw him going off to sea in a power-boat.'

'Going off to sea?' Captain Hart was astounded. 'I sent a message for him to come here immediately.'

'I'm sorry, sir. But that's what the rating told me. The Doctor seemed to be going after another power-boat.'

'The Master!' Jo exclaimed. 'Can't you see what's happened?'

'I can see very clearly,' said Mr. Walker. 'Your Doctor has gone over to the other side.' He turned to Captain Hart. 'I am giving you the following order, Captain. Strike, and strike hard, and do it *now*, using an underwater nuclear warhead. Obey my command, or face a charge of insubordination.'

Captain Hart looked at Jo. 'I'm sorry, Miss Grant. I shall have to do what I'm told.'

.   .   .   .   .

In a workshop section of the Sea-Devils' base, many fathoms below the surface, the Doctor again found himself being forced to help the Master complete the reactivation device. A Sea-Devil guard remained with them, its raygun pointed at the Doctor.

'I still don't understand why you want to help them,' the Doctor said quietly as they worked.

'Revenge,' said the Master, 'against the entire human race. It was they who sentenced me to life-long imprisonment.'

'It was they,' said the Doctor, 'who did *not* sentence you to death. They had good reason to execute you. Instead, they showed mercy.'

'For that,' said the Master, adding another component to the already complex device. 'I was truly grateful—while I was a prisoner. But now that I'm free, I can think clearly. And I want revenge!' He looked across curiously at the work the Doctor was doing. 'What are you up to?'

'Carrying out your commands,' said the Doctor. 'You told me to deal with the polarity of the neutron flow.'

The Master crossed to where the Doctor was working, and looked at the complicated component which he had just attached to the device. 'Yes, that seems all right. You're working very well.'

'Thank you,' said the Doctor. 'I think that completes the job.'

Another Sea-Devil entered the workshop. 'I am now the new leader,' it said slowly. 'When will you complete your task? We wish to re-activate our kin throughout this planet!'

'I'm pleased to report,' said the Master, 'that I have just finished.' He added with a chuckle, 'With the help of my slave, of course.'

The new Chief Sea-Devil regarded the device. 'Then put it into operation.'

'Delighted,' said the Master. 'Please stand back, Doctor.'

The Doctor stood away from the device, and the Master switched on the main electrical current. The device started to hum gently.

'You realise,' said the Doctor, 'that it will take some hours for the power to build up.'

The Master ignored the Doctor's remark, and addressed himself to the Chief Sea-Devil. 'Within a short time from now you will begin to receive signals from your other shelters and bases as they start to revive from their hibernation. Since we no longer need the Doctor, I suggest you put him into one of your cages.'

'I agree,' said the Chief Sea-Devil. It raised its hand and three Sea-Devil guards entered. 'Put these creatures into the cages. Don't kill them yet, not until we are sure that their device works.'

The guards grabbed both the Doctor *and* the Master.

'Don't be ridiculous,' the Master protested. 'I am your friend. We made a pact.'

'We make no pacts with apes,' said the Chief Sea-Devil. 'Take them away!'

'I am a Time Lord,' screamed the Master as the guards dragged him away. 'They will destroy you!'

The Doctor walked quietly with the guards to the prison area of the shelter. Ahead in the seemingly endless corridors, the Master struggled between two Sea-Devils, and was partly dragged to the cages. They were put into the same cage, the door was locked, and the Sea-Devils went away. The Master grabbed at the bars of the cage and shouted: 'I am the Master! I demand to be released!'

There was no answer.

'You seem to have lost your touch,' said the Doctor quietly.

The Master turned on him, his eyes blazing. 'Once they see that the device really works, they will release me!'

'I doubt it,' said the Doctor. 'Just before you switched on, I reversed the polarity of the neutron flow.'

The Master was appalled. 'You did *what*? There'll be a reverse feed-back into their entire power system! This whole shelter will explode. We'll be killed!'

'That's right,' said the Doctor, 'in about ten minutes from now.'

The Master turned back to the gaping hole of the corridor they had been brought down. 'Guards! Come back! You've got to release me!'

'Even if they listened to you,' continued the Doctor calmly, 'which I doubt if they will, it would be no good. I built a destructor mechanism into the major control switch. It cannot now be turned off.' He felt into his coat pocket and brought out his sonic screwdriver. 'Now, if you will stand away from that lock, my friend, let's see what we can do.'

'Even if you can open that lock,' said the Master, 'what then? We'd drown before we ever got to the surface.'

'Not necessarily,' said the Doctor. He pointed the sonic screwdriver at the lock. From inside the lock they heard a number of clicks, as the internal bars and levers fell back into the unlocked position. 'There, that seems to have done it.' He pulled open the door. 'Now follow me and do exactly what I tell you.'

The Doctor led the Master to where the Sea-Devils had dumped equipment taken from the submarine. They seemed to have lifted out everything removable, including the submarine's escape apparatuses. The Doctor selected two sets of oxygen canisters, harnesses, and face masks. 'Get that on,' he ordered, and the Master obeyed without question.

'How do we get out of there?' said the Master, strapping on the harness.

'The way we came in,' said the Doctor. 'There must be an airlock somewhere—the place they brought us in in those pods. Now follow me.'

As they hurried away from the cages to seek the airlock, the humming sound of the sabotaged re-activation device began to fill the entire underwater shelter.

.   .   .   .   .

Fifty feet above the choppy surface of the sea, young Lieutenant Scott held his helicopter in a hovering position. His petty officer navigator looked down at the surface.

'What are we supposed to be looking for, sir?' asked the petty officer.

'One, possibly two, men,' replied Lieutenant Scott. He looked to a point about a mile away from the oil-rig. A light cruiser was coming in fast. He knew it carried underwater nuclear missiles. Captain Hart had told Scott to do whatever he could to save the Doctor before the missiles were dropped.

'Down there!' shouted the petty officer. 'There's two of them!'

Lieutenant Scott looked straight below where two heads were bobbing about in the water. 'Get winching,' he told his petty officer, then gently lowered the helicopter to within a few feet of the surface. The petty officer threw out the cradle on its long line, and lowered it to within inches of the Master. The Master grabbed at the cradle, heaving himself up out of the water. The petty officer set the electric winch in motion, and wound up the cradle towards the belly of the helicopter. Reaching out, he grabbed the Master's hand and pulled him inboard. Then he dropped the cradle again to the Doctor. A minute later the Doctor, too, was scrambling inboard.

'Welcome on board,' shouted Lieutenant Scott. He pointed to the light cruiser. 'Just in time, too. That thing's going to blast those monsters into another world.'

'It won't be necessary,' said the Doctor. 'At least, I don't think so.'

Before his words were fully uttered, the sea below them started to boil as a huge explosion took place many fathoms below. The sea rose up in a great mountain of water, foaming white on top, then slowly subsided.

'Very clever of you,' said the Master. 'Do you realise you have just committed mass murder?'

The Doctor looked down at the seething waters as the helicopter turned and flew them back to safety. He said nothing. What the Master had just said was true.

.   .   .   .   .

Jo, Captain Hart and Mr. Walker were all waiting at the Naval Base's heliport as the helicopter slowly dropped down to land. There was an ambulance standing by, with two ambulance men ready with a stretcher. The helicopter landed, and the first out was the Doctor, followed by Lieutenant Scott.

'Well done,' said Captain Hart. 'What's this about the Master?'

'He collapsed in the helicopter,' said the Doctor, 'that's why I radio'd for you to have an ambulance standing by.'

The two ambulance men rushed forward to the helicopter and took their stretcher inside.

'What about these monsters?' Walker demanded.

'I destroyed their base for you,' the Doctor explained. 'As the Master so delicately put it, I murdered them.'

'Excellent,' said Walker. 'I knew you would see it my way in the end.'

'I did what I had to do,' said the Doctor, 'to prevent a war. I don't want your thanks.'

By now the two ambulance men were coming from the helicopter carrying the stretcher. A blanket was drawn over the form on the stretcher, even covering the face.

'He's dead,' said Jo, in awe, 'the Master is dead.'

'We were too late,' said one of the ambulance men. 'The doctor in the helicopter said he died of a heart attack.'

The Doctor whipped back the blanket from the stretcher. Lying there in a state of hypnosis was the petty officer navigator. He opened his eyes. 'I must obey the Master . . . I must obey . . .'

The engine of the helicopter roared into life. The Doctor swung round to see the Master seated at the controls. The Master smiled, and gave the Doctor a wave. Then he took off, and flew away.

'This is outrageous,' exploded Mr. Walker. 'We must send up fighter planes to shoot him down immediately. He must be caught at all costs!'

The Doctor tried to conceal a wry smile. 'I don't think it will do any good, Mr. Walker. Something tells me we are not going to see the Master again—at least, not until he wants us to.'

'DOCTOR WHO'

Δ	0426200497	IAN MARTER Doctor Who and the Sontaren Experiment	60p
Δ	0426110331	MALCOLM HULKE Doctor Who and the Space War	85p
Δ	0426200993	TERRANCE DICKS Doctor Who and the Stones of Blood	75p
Δ	0426119738	TERRANCE DICKS Doctor Who and the Talons of Weng Chiang	75p
Δ	0426115007	Doctor Who and the Terror of the Autons	75p
Δ	0426200233	Doctor Who and the Time Warrior	75p
Δ	0426200233	GERRY DAVIS Doctor Who and the Tomb of the Cybermen	75p
Δ	0426200683	TERRANCE DICKS Doctor Who and the Underworld	75p
Δ	0426200683	TERRANCE DICKS Doctor Who and the Web of Fear	75p
Δ	0426110412	TERRANCE DICKS Doctor Who and the Loch Ness Monster	85p
Δ	0426118936	PHILIP HINCHCLIFFE Doctor Who and the Masque of Mandragora	85p
Δ	0426116909	TERRANCE DICKS Doctor Who and the Mutants	75p
Δ	0426201302	Doctor Who and the Nightmare of Eden	85p
Δ	0426112520	Doctor Who and the Planet of the Daleks	75p

DOCTOR WHO

Δ	0426116828	Doctor Who and the Planet of Evil	75p
Δ	0426106555	Dr Who and the Planet of the Spiders	85p
Δ	0426201019	Doctor Who and the Power of Kroll	85p
Δ	0426116666	Doctor Who and the Pyramids of Mars	75p
Δ	0426116585	PHILIP HINCHCLIFFE Doctor Who and the Seeds of Doom	85p
	0426200675	TERRANCE DICKS The Adventures of K9 and other Mechanical Creatures (illus)	75p
	0426200950	Terry Nation's Dalek Special (illus)	95p
	0426114477	Doctor Who Monster Book (Colour illus)	50p
	0426200012	The Second Doctor Who Monster Book (Colour illus)	70p
	0426118421	Doctor Who Dinosaur Book (illus)	75p
	0426200020	Doctor Who Discovers Prehistoric Animals (NF) (illus)	75p
	0426200039	Doctor Who Discovers Space Travel (NF) (illus)	75p
	042620004/	Doctor Who Discovers Strange and Mysterious Creatures (NF) (illus)	75p
	042620008X	Doctor Who Discovers the Story of Early Man (NF) (illus)	75p
	0426200136	Doctor Who Discovers the Conquerors (NF) (illus)	75p
	0426116151	TERRANCE DICKS AND MALCOLM HULKE The Making of Doctor Who	95p

DOCTOR WHO

Δ	0426200969	Doctor Who and the Destiny of the Daleks	75p
Δ	0426108744	MALCOLM HULKE Doctor Who and the Dinosaur Invasion	75p
Δ	0426103726	Doctor Who and the Doomsday Weapon	85p
Δ	0426200063	TERRANCE DICKS Doctor Who and the Face of Evil	85p
Δ	0426112601	Doctor Who and the Genesis of The Daleks	75p
Δ	0426112792	Doctor Who and the Giant Robot	85p
Δ	0426115430	MALCOLM HULKE Doctor Who and the Green Death	75p
Δ	0426200330	TERRANCE DICKS Doctor Who and the Hand of Fear	75p
Δ	0426201310	Doctor Who and the Horns of Nimon	85p
Δ	0426200772	Doctor Who and the Image of The Fendahl	75p
Δ	0426200934	Doctor Who and the Invasion of Time	75p
Δ	0426200543	Doctor Who and the Invisible Enemy	75p
Δ	0426201256	PHILIP HINCHCLIFFE Doctor Who and the Keys of Marinus	85p

If you enjoyed this book and would like to have information sent to you about other TARGET titles, write to the address below.

You will also receive:
A FREE TARGET BADGE!
Based on the TARGET BOOKS symbol — see front cover of this book — this attractive three-colour badge, pinned to your blazer-lapel or jumper, will excite the interest and comment of all your friends!

and you will be further entitled to:
FREE ENTRY INTO THE TARGET DRAW!
All you have to do is cut off the coupon below, write on it your name and address in *block capitals,* and pin it to your letter. Twice a year, in June, and December, coupons will be drawn 'from the hat' and the winner will receive a complete year's set of TARGET books.

Write to:

TARGET BOOKS
44 Hill Street
London W1X 8LB

cut here

Full name . . . .

Address. . . . .

. . . .

. . . .

Age. . . . .

PLEASE ENCLOSE A SELF-ADDRESSED STAMPED ENVELOPE WITH YOUR COUPON!